The Goddess in Love with a Horse

The Goddess in Love with a Horse

(And What Happened Next)

Eugene Mirabelli

Spring Harbor Press

ISBN 978-0-935891-09-6
Library of Congress Control Number: 2008923256

Published by Spring Harbor Press in 2008
Spring Harbor Press is part of Spring Harbor, Ltd.
Box 346, Delmar, New York, 12054
www.springharborpress.com

Cover by Ed Atkeson of Berg Design
Book design by Seagull Graphics
Printed on acid-free paper

Spring Harbor Books may be ordered from the publisher:
Box 346, Delmar, New York, 12054.
Add two dollars for media postage and handling.
New York State residents add sales tax.
Visit us online at www.springharborpress.com.

The author thanks Antonio D'Alfonso, founder of the distinguished Guernica Editions, for publishing *The World at Noon*, the novel in which progenitors of the Cavallù family first appeared. In addition, *The American Poetry Review*, *The Michigan Quarterly Review*, *Arba Sicula* and *Fantasy & Science Fiction* helped to establish the Cavallù genealogy, as did the editors of the *Sweet Lemons* anthology.

for Margaret
& the children
& the children's children

Note from the Narrator

Everything in this book is true. The story of Angelo Cavallù (man from the waist up, horse from the waist down) is unlikely, but so is the invention of the aeroplane which also takes place in these pages. The plain factual history of Sicily is unbelievably awful, terrible, horrible and heartbreaking, but true. Boston is a real place, so is the North End.

1

THE FIRST TIME AVA SAW ANGELO NAKED was on their wedding night (11 May 1860) when he strode into their bedroom, accidentally revealing to her startled eyes that from the waist down he had the hindquarters of a stallion. Now Angelo was no brute. He was a miller and this was in his house in Carco, Sicily. He had knocked gently and he and thought he heard her whisper Come in, but when he opened the door the room was ablaze with candles and Ava was still on her knees in prayer at the bedside. She lifted her head and saw — Angelo was wearing only the fancy shirt he had married in — saw those supreme flanks, hocks, fetlocks and horny soled feet. The blood drained from her face. For a moment she wavered and flickered, then she murmured the last words of her Hail Mary, blessed herself and stood up. "Amen," Angelo said, taking her cool hand in his. "I have something to tell you."

"Your legs —" she began.

"Remember," Angelo broke in. "God created horses, too. In fact, horses are among the most noble of God's creatures. Horses aren't soaked in blood. They don't have fangs or claws. They don't kill and they don't eat other horses. Horses are peaceful, more peaceful than men, not cowardly like sheep or stupid like oxen, but serene and powerful. God created horses just to show us what He could do in the way of power and beauty, and when He finished, He admired His handiwork. He admires horses. Horses have strength and grace and intelligence, horses have courage and endurance, horses have fidelity. Besides, I'm not wholly, not —"

"Your bottom half —" she began again.

"There've been other unions, but they were horrible mismatches and produced mongrel beasts. Harpies, manticores, bull-headed minotaurs. Only Chiron, the centaur, was a scholar and teacher. Besides, as I said —"

"Your thing —" she began once more.

"Don't let the great size frighten you." His voice was gentle, almost complacent.

"A horse?" she asked, astounded.

"A stallion," he said. He was quite frank about it. Sicily was a beautiful land where strange and terrible things happened every day of the week.

"I will not bed down with a horse!" Ava snatched her hand from his and ran around to the far side of the bed and stood there, watching him.

"It's been a long day and we're both tired," Angelo

said, keeping quite still so as not to frighten her.

"So?"

"And when we're tired we should go to sleep."

"I'm never going to sleep. Certainly not with you," she said, her voice trembling.

"You look so fierce," Angelo remarked, simply to make her feel better. He had begun to stroll very slowly down the room on his side of the bed. "You look —"

"Not tonight, not tomorrow night, not ever!"

"Wild" he continued. "Like an animal. I like that, of course. An animal." He paused at the foot of the bed and smiled at her. "You are a magnificent woman."

Ava had almost started to say something but now she hesitated, her lips still parted, distracted by what he had just said.

"A splendid woman," he continued. "It's hard to believe that when I first saw you your legs were so thin I thought they would snap in two. You were always running after your aunt and everywhere she went you would follow her, trotting after her like a foal."

"Because I was ten years old," she protested.

"And now you are a woman of seventeen with beautiful teeth and strong round arms. And, I imagine, sturdy legs. We will be superb at making love."

Ava clapped her hands over her ears.

Angelo laughed. He praised her hair — told her it shimmered like a river at midnight — then spoke quietly about her luminous eyes, her gleaming

3

shoulders something, her something breasts, and so on downward, dropping his voice softer and softer, so that Ava who had opened her fingers just a bit to hear him had to open them more and still more until, straining to catch his last words, she forgot herself and said, "What? What flower? — Stop! Don't come any closer!"

"Calm yourself," Angelo said. He seated himself on the low chest which stood against the wall by the foot of the bed. "How long do you plan to stand over there?" he asked.

"As long as I want to."

"Of course. But why not sit on the bed? Filomena scented the sheets with lavender, just for us."

Ava seated herself guardedly on the edge of the bed, watching him all the time.

"This is a pretty room, isn't it?" he said, looking around. "I whitewashed it myself a week ago." In fact, it was a pretty room. In addition to the bed there was a low dresser, a rush-bottomed chair, and in the space between two shuttered windows there was a washstand with an oval mirror hung above it. Angelo said, "The candles look nice, too. I didn't expect you to light them all at once, but they do look nice. Like a church at High Mass. Maybe that's why I'm so sleepy. Church always makes me sleepy," he confessed. "Or maybe it's my age. I'm no child and at my age —"

"What are you doing?" Ava cried, jumping up.

"I'm unbuttoning my shirt. I'm going to bed."

"Bed? What bed? Stop!"

But Angelo was already on his feet, rampant, and now he threw off his shirt, letting it billow onto the chair, and there he stood naked while a dozen shadows of him reared and plunged on the whitewashed wall at his back. Ava had started to cover her eyes but it was too late. Now she simply looked at him and the candle flames grew calm again and the shadows grew still. His flesh was a rich chestnut color and his hair was black — black on his head, black in his beard, black everywhere. His shoulders gleamed, at the base of his throat there was a little hollow filled with golden shadow and on his chest the pattern of hair spread like the wings of a crow. His navel was deep and dark, his legs — ah, those splendid stallion legs — his flanks so smoothly muscled that as he walked the flesh shimmered, and the short downy hairs on his rump, the curling hairs on his thighs, the tassel-like hairs on his fetlocks, all sparkled like coal, and in the center, of course, as if the darkness of night had taken beastly shape — But Angelo was blowing out the candles one by one and it was becoming harder to see. He stopped when there was only the solitary chamber stick burning on the chest of drawers. Then he leapt into bed, stacked two pillows behind his back and sat with the sheets pulled to his chest. He looked at Ava. "I'm going to sleep," he said.

"I'm not sleepy."

"Would you like to rest on the top of the covers?"

She came and sat on the edge of the bed, her back to him.

"Give me your hand," he said.

"What are you going to do?" she asked, half turning.

"I'm going to sit here like we used to sit on the bench in your aunt's garden. What did we ever do there? Now give me your hand."

"All right," she said. She lay back on the covers against him and got comfortable. "But don't try to reason with me," she added.

"Of course not." He put his arms about her and took her hands. "Now that we're married, there's a secret I can tell you."

"I already know your secret," she said.

"Now listen. This is what you don't know. When a man of my kind, a man of my nature — when a man who is part stallion makes love to a woman, she inherits three gifts."

"Everything I ever inherited is in that ugly chest."

"These gifts come because he makes love to her. They come with his lovemaking, with his —" Angelo hesitated, hunting for the proper word.

"What three gifts?"

"Her childbirths will be easy, her milk will be sweet, and she will be beautiful forever."

"Angelo, you liar." She laughed.

"These talents will be yours by nature," he continued, undeflected. "And they'll be passed on to our daughters and their daughters, too, if we make love often enough."

"And the boys? What would they inherit?"

"My sons will be like me, of course." His breath was soft behind her ear. He went on talking in a voice gentle and resonant and even dreamy, speaking of his father and mother and the village where they lay, which was deep in the heart of Sicily, and in the hour or so that followed he told about those spirits hidden in the hills and fields around the village, told about the patron saints and beasts and, while his voice grew even sleepier, he talked about his relatives, not all of whom were horse, for one was a famous tree and another was a rock and there was an aunt —"

"Yes?" Ava said, turning to him. "Go on. I'm listening."

But Angelo was asleep. She turned all the way around and crept cautiously over the covers to study his face: his beard, his lips, the hard wrinkles at the corner of his eyes. A handsome man, she thought. His breathing was deep and slow, for he was fast asleep, but the guttering candle made the shadows on his face waver as if he were stirring and about to wake up. So Ava lay on the covers and listened to his soft, slow breathing and watched the candle flicker out and strove to keep awake.

Angelo awoke early and found Ava sleeping like a statue at his side atop the bed covers. He gazed at her in the milky light, at her flushed cheeks and parted lips — how young she was! — cautiously lifted his hand to caress her, but changed his mind and slipped softly out of bed. In the dim hall he pulled on his workpants and boots, then groped his way down the dark stairs to wash in the courtyard. He hoped that a brisk walk on the hills would relieve the painful energy compressed in his legs, his thighs. He pulled on his shirt and flung open the gate and abruptly a horse and rider materialized out of the gray air. "He has landed," the rider told him.

"Ah!" Angelo said.

"Yesterday at Marsala."

Angelo wheeled and ran back into the court-yard, pounded once on the stable door, once on the kitchen door, then clattered up the stairway to his bedroom. "Garibaldi has landed at Marsala and I'm going to join him!" he cried, throwing off his shirt. Ava reached for the latch on the window shutters, staring at him. Angelo sat on the bed to pull off his boots and pants, then flung on his wedding shirt and strode out to the hall. He returned clothed in the fancy shirt and his best pair of velveteen pants. "I have waited all my life for this," he said, pulling on his boots. He crossed the room to Ava who stood by the open window, still staring at him. "You're crazy," she said soberly. Angelo took both her hands in his and kissed her lips. "Remember that I love you," he told her.

"Garibaldi is an animal, a beast," she said, her voice rising.

He laughed. "Then he has come to the right place."

"We will die," she wailed.

"We have always died. But today you should be singing."

Ava wrenched her hands from his and began to beat her fists on his chest, shouting "Go, go, go, go, go —" She had broken into sobs.

"I have never been so happy," he said, putting his arms around this sturdy young woman who wept for him.

Angelo kissed the crown of her head and rushed down the stairway to the dining room. There he tossed back the lid of a black oak chest, peeled away the linens and flannels and came up with an antique bird gun, then he strode into the yard, pulling a heavy pistol from under the big flower pot by the door, and was shouting *Filomena* as he crossed to the stable where the boy had saddled the gelding. He mounted, took the bundle of food which Filomena handed up to him — leftovers from the wedding wrapped in oilcloth — and went out through the gate at a canter, leaving the boy at the stable door, Filomena in the middle of the yard, his uncles and half-brothers asleep indoors, and his virgin bride face down on her bed, beating her pillow.

Garibaldi had landed on the western shore of Sicily and everyone knew what he had come to do. He was a simple man with a simple desire. He would drive the King's troops first from that great island and then from the Kingdom of Naples and the forlorn southern peninsula, so that these lands could join with those in the north and become one Italy, a single nation as it had been ages ago. The King had 24,864 well-equipped troops waiting in Sicily. Garibaldi had come ashore with only 1,000 volunteers, some in red shirts and others in street clothes, and for guns they had junk — antique smooth-bore muskets, 100 Enfield rifles and 5 ancient cannons without gun carriages. At dawn the next morning he walked his patched-together army inland through seas of green corn and beans to Rampagallo, and the following day he trudged with them past silvery groves of olive trees up to the sun-baked highlands of Salemi. They spent the night in Salemi, some in houses and others in monasteries and still others under tents in the orchards outside. The next day their numbers increased a bit as volunteer squadre came up from the countryside, armed with flintlocks or pruning hooks, and somewhere among them was Angelo, Angelo Cavallù, *our* Angelo. He was dusty, for his horse had collapsed of exhaustion and Angelo had trotted over the hills and into town on his own two feet. That afternoon he saw Garibaldi dismount, stroll across a corner of the piazza and pass through a doorway: a pleasant-looking man with a rich honey-color beard, clothed in a loose red shirt — a man who moved with the effortless grace of an animal. Garibaldi was content at that moment, for he had just ridden in from a survey of the ground along the road to Palermo and now he was going to study a big map of Sicily which one of his officers had found.

Until then he had not had a good map. That night, when he folded the map and went to bed, rain had begun to fall, but when he awoke at three the next morning the rain had ceased and it was beautiful. He pulled on his pants, drank a cup of coffee, called in his officers, told them what he planned to do and sent them to rouse his little army. He had been walking up and down the room and now he burst into song. Here was a fifty-three-year-old man about to attack an army of vastly superior numbers in a battle in which defeat meant death and he sang like a lover going to meet his mistress, because he was about to have his heart's desire.

That morning Angelo marched with the squadre down the road and through a valley where everyone bought oranges and lemons, then they left the road and trudged up a stony hillside. From the top of their bald hill they looked across a shallow alley to a steeper, terraced hill on top of which brightly uniformed troops were gathered in squares — there and there and there and there and over there. They were too many. Angelo's disheartened squadre, which had never been in a battle before, drifted quietly off to the side to watch how it was done. Over there, General Sforza ordered his trumpets to sound and ranks of identical soldiers began to step down the hill, to wade across the stream at the bottom and mount toward the volunteers, firing as they came. Over here, a bugler blew that fancy musical reveille which Garibaldi loved so much and a handful of his skirmishers began to fire at the oncoming troops. Of

11

their own accord, the rest of Garibaldi's men, who had been sitting on the stony rubbish high on the hill, stood up — men in red shirts, men in street jackets, some even in top hats — and now they were running down at the troops in a burst of musketry. Angelo galloped after them. The Garibaldini drove the army back across the stream and part way up the terraced hillside. Then everything slowed. The afternoon grew slack and there was only the irregular clatter of gunfire, or once in a while the top of the enemy hill blossomed into white puffs of smoke and cannonballs shrieked past, and the sun roamed aimlessly overhead. It grew hot, terribly hot. Every so often Garibaldi's red-shirts were driven down, or they climbed further up, but their numbers always diminished and now there were not so many — in fact, there were only a few hundred crouched on the steep hillside, pressed together here and there beneath the ragged terraces. Angelo sat with his shoulder against his own bit of loose stone wall, sucking the juice from his last orange, and he peered higher up the hill to where Garibaldi huddled with his bare sword and a crowd of his outlandish army. The terrace wall they clung to was nearest the summit and royalist troops were firing volley after volley down on them, even throwing rocks. He is a lion, thought Angelo, but I am only part of a horse and maybe not the best part at that. What do we do now? A rock hit Garibaldi on the back and he stood up, his sword flashing. His men stood up beside him. Now Garibaldi was climbing the terrace, his men were climbing the terrace. They were rising up everywhere on the hillside, rising and climbing through the ragged noise, crawling higher and higher, clawing up over the last heap of stones into a hazy white smoke filled with crackling gunfire and screams. Then there was the long hilltop slanting off and royalist troops running away, streaming down and away to the far valley, fleeing.

＊ ＊ ＊ ＊ ＊

Angelo marched here and there and elsewhere with Garibaldi for two weeks while the old fox outwitted the King's generals and drove the royal army from Sicily, then Angelo walked home. He wore a stained slouch hat and such tattered velveteen that when he turned in at the gate only his dog, Micu, recognized who it was, circling him and barking excitedly and leaping while Filomena and the boy stared. His bride cried, "Angelo!" from an upstairs window, "Angelo!" from the doorway, "Angelo!" as she threw her arms around his neck. He kissed her forehead and each cheek and said, "Tell Filomena to start heating water because I am going to take a long, long bath."

In the house they poured pots of steaming water into the copper tub which Angelo had dragged to the side of the bed. Ava laid out the towels, brush and soap on the table between the windows and turned to go, but Angelo took her wrist in one hand and gently closed the door with his other. Without a word he shed his shirt, pulled off his boots and stepped out of his pants. Ava stood at the window, staring out, and heard his gasp as he lowered himself into the scalding water.

"I cannot wash my own back," he said in a reasonable voice.

Ava turned hesitantly, a light flush on her cheeks, and took the soap and brush from the table and knelt behind his back. She lifted a cupped handful of water and let it trickle onto his shoulder, then another handful and another and one more. She dipped the soap into the water and slid it tenderly all the way across his back from the tip of one shoulder to the tip of the other. "Ah, that's good," Angelo murmured. Ava pressed her wet palm to his warm back and rubbed in a circle, making suds. "The first time I saw Garibaldi I was so close I could have reached out and touched him," he told her. "He's an old man, older than I am, but he moves very lightly, like an animal. — Would you like me to tell you what I've been doing for two weeks?" Ava dipped the soap into the water and swept it up and down his marvelous, silken back, enjoying herself. "Yes. Tell me," she said absently.

Later, when he had finished with his stories and his bath, Angelo stepped from the tub, letting the water sluice from him in streams as if he were a mountain, then he toweled himself dry and fell asleep in his bed for a day and a night. He dreamed.

Maybe the dreams came from his aching muscles or the marrow of his bones or maybe they came from his blood, which was, after all, the mingled blood of men and beasts, of Siculi and Greeks, Romans, Carthaginians, Byzantines, Arabs, Jews, Normans, Spaniards — in other words, *pure* Sicilian blood. Occasionally his magnificent legs twitched and he gave a deep resonant groan, because he was dreaming not only his own story but the cruel three-thousand-year history of all Sicily. He was having a nightmare. At last he awoke and in the pale blue dawn he found Ava sleeping at his side, on top of the covers, an arm flung over her head and her hair spread loose upon the pillow.

He kissed her lips. Before she could rub the sleep from her eyes, Angelo said, "Come with me. I'll show you the world in the morning." He began to open the shutters. Ava stood there in her white chemise and watched him as the room filled up with light. She wanted to look at those equine hindquarters, those powerful flanks and long shins, wanted to see the dark whorls of hair on his chest, the satin nap on his underbelly, his black pouch and stallion thing. His flesh was the color of bronze and smooth beneath her fingertips as a chestnut fresh from its hull. Suddenly he knelt and scooped up the hem of her chemise, standing and lifting it so rapidly that she barely had time to raise her arms before the garment was unfurling in air, falling into a shadowy corner of the room. He put a warm hand on her haunch and when she lowered her eyes he kissed the nape of

15

her neck. Now he whispered a few words in her ear and she tossed her head back, laughing. Who knows what happened next? Her births were always easy, her milk was always sweet, and she remained beautiful into old age. Their daughters inherited these traits. Their sons had legs like their father.

2

N

O ONE HAS BEEN ABLE TO WRITE a complete
history of Sicily. Every historian who tries,
fails — they sink into bewilderment or go
mad with rage or collapse in grief, weeping. The
agony that is Sicilian history is too terrible to think
about. Ages ago Greeks with swords and chains in-
vaded the island paradise and wrote about the locals
who had cleared the forests and were farming. That's
the last glimpse we get of Sicilians living free. In
the next two thousand and six hundred years one
greedy army after another came ashore to kill, im-
prison and brutalize them. After taking over, the
new land-owners inscribed laws, contracts, leases
and taxes on the flesh of the poor to enrich themselves and to immiserate the landless, so that each
impoverished family had to turn against all others to survive. Some of the dispossessed went back
to the caves of their ancestors, and others lived in
the fields with nothing but the tattered clothes they
wore to show they were people, not beasts. By 1860
a handful of idle nobles and their henchmen owned
almost the whole island, receiving their legitimacy
from the Bourbon King who sat in Naples, across
the water in Italy. That was the year Angelo married
Ava in May, the same month that Giuseppe Garib-

aldi landed on Sicily's western shore with a thousand volunteers. Garibaldi swept eastward to the great city of Palermo and from there to the eastern edge of the island, the city of Messina. On the shore at Messina you can look across the water to the city of Reggio Calabria situated on the southernmost tip of Italy. The city lies just above the watery horizon and behind it the brown, sun-dried land rises toward the harsh mountains beyond. In the old city of Reggio, off the main avenue, on one of the narrow side streets, there used to be a house – to speak plainly, a whore house, a bordello – called the Conca d'Oro (the Golden Shell), a well kept house with accommodating women, a friendly place.

3

THE FIRST TIME FRANCO WATCHED STELLA undress (20 August 1860) in her room at the bordello Conca d'Oro, her freshness and beauty struck him so hard that he fell to his knees, opened his arms and asked her to marry him. "I've never seen anyone so beautiful and I love you," he said. Stella looked at him, her face as serene as polished marble, and began slowly to unpin her hair. The room was filled with dusky golden light which filtered through the shuttered windows. "Marry me," he whispered. "Marry me," She held the pin in her teeth and calmly watched him while her hands searched in the coiled mass of her hair and when she had found the last one she laid all the pins in a sea shell on the bed table. She had worked a few years and was no longer surprised at the way men behaved in her room. "What do I say?" she asked distantly.

"Say yes."

"Yes," she recited, her loosened hair turning languidly about her breast and arm, unrolling over her wrist, across her thigh.

"Diva," the young man murmured. "Goddess."

"Yes. I am a goddess." She was matter-of-fact about it. Of course, the people of southern Italy never made much of the difference between mortals and gods, and you never knew when a man might become a god, or a goddess become a woman, or vice versa.

Franco knelt slowly forward and kissed her feet, embraced her legs as if gathering an armful of long-stemmed flowers, and plunged his face into her dark—

"But first you must wash," Stella told him, firmly turning his hot cheek aside so that he might see the big white pitcher and bowl on a very low little table. "Over there," she said. Franco staggered to his feet, his head filled with the odor of lemon flowers and brine. He poured the water into the bowl, set the pitcher down with a hollow clink on the marble, and began to scrub his face. "Not your face! Not in *that!*" Stella cried.

Franco straightened up and turned, water streaming from his bare shoulders and chest onto his trousers. "What?"

"Not your *face*, caro. Wash—" Stella sighed and took up the towel that lay folded on the table and began to dry his chin. "You're new here?" she asked.

Franco was distracted by her nakedness so near to him, by the way her long hair fell upon her breasts, turned about her arm and uncoiled heavily to her knees. "Yes!" he said, getting his wits together. He told her he came from a village in the Calabrian mountains, but that he had traveled around and picked up an education and, as a matter of fact, in a short time he was going off to teach mathematics.

He said he believed in mathematics and he thought he would like teaching it. Just now he was down here in Reggio — "the home of Pythagoras," he noted — merely to stroll around and enjoy the cafés and views of the sea. This Reggio was a city of vistas and he had discovered he was crazy about looking at the sea. Then he unbuckled and, because he was shy, turned his back to her before he stepped out of his pants.

"Maybe you'll see the Fata Morgana," Stella said, coming around to watch him. "The castles float in the air far above the water. It's famous."

"An optical illusion, a mirage," Franco said, hurriedly soaping himself.

"Of course it's an illusion. Morgana conjures the castles out of thin air. That's why it's called Fata Morgana, because she's the one who creates it."

"I'm a rationalist," he informed her. "I'm a freethinker and a mathematician and I don't believe in — What are you looking at?" he asked, covering his drenched privates with his hand.

"Don't worry. It won't fly away. Here's a towel." She walked idly to the shuttered window and peered between the slats at the balcony and at the sunny strip of street below. "I don't know anything about rationalists or freethinkers, but the Royalists don't like them. Have you seen all the soldiers?"

"They don't frighten me."

"They say Garibaldi has come over from Sicily."

"They've been saying that for weeks."

"How long have you been here in Reggio?" she asked, peeping again through the shutters to the

21

sunny balcony.

"Three days," he said. "How long have you been at the Conca d'Oro?"

For a while she did not answer. "Forever, I think."

"That's not true."

Stella turned to him as if she were weary, the golden light spreading up like a fan behind her. "All my life, this life, I've been here."

Franco studied her face to see what she meant, but in that topaz shadow he could never make it out. She seemed made of honey-colored marble and so remote he felt half afraid of her. "You are the most beautiful woman I've ever seen," he whispered.

Stella smiled. "Yes. I'm a goddess. And you are a very young man — a rationalist, a freethinker and a mathematician." And taking Franco's hand she led him to her bed, drew up her long legs and sank back upon the white pillows as if bedded in clouds.

Franco was young and enthusiastic and they made love for a long, long time, but even with a goddess it comes to an end — unless you are a god, which Franco was not. Stella arose and went to the big mirror that stood by the bed and Franco, leaning up on his elbow, watched her draw on her blue silk robe.

"If you were my wife —" he began.

"I wouldn't respect you. How could I respect anyone foolish enough to marry a whore?" She was brushing her hair in long slow strokes.

"I believe in the future, not the past. I don't care what you've done."

"Because you don't know what I've done. If you want to marry me you must come back tonight and watch me at work."

"Are you serious?" he asked.

"You can hide on the balcony and watch through the shutters." She took a pin from the fluted sea shell on her bed table and began to coil her hair upon her head.

"And then —"

"Afterward, you must tell me everything you saw," she said.

"Why?"

"So I'll know that you really watched. And then —"

"Then I'll ask you to marry me," said Franco, swinging himself from the bed.

"Then you won't ask," said Stella.

Franco returned early that night. The room looked just the same as it had that afternoon, but now there was an oil lamp burning on the low table beside the wash basin and Stella had her hair up in a large braided knot.

"Did you think I'd come back?" he asked cheerfully.

"Yes," she said.

Stella set a bottle of brandy and two glasses on the low table. She was wearing a white dress which left her golden shoulders and arms bare to the hazy lamplight. She poured out the brandy and they each took up a glass.

"My name is Franco Morelli and I live in our

house in the town of Morano in Cosenza," he announced.

Stella looked at him in surprise. "My name is Stella Maria DiMare and I live in the bordello Conca d'Oro in Reggio, Calabria." She smiled.

They touched glasses and drank.

"You're a handsome young man. Did your mother ever tell you that?" she asked.

"I don't know. My mother died when I was a child."

"Oh. I'm sorry. My own mother died when I was born," she added.

"My father is a carpenter and cabinet maker."

"And my father was a fisherman," she said. Stella smiled, remembering him. "He used to tell me that he found me at sea. Other children were found under cabbages, but he used to say that he pulled in his nets one morning and there I was, swimming with all the fishes. I loved that story. He used to carry me on his shoulders. He died in 1848. I think it was during the bombardment. He sailed out and never came back."

Stella sat on the foot of her bed, Franco sat in a stiff chair, and they talked and talked, getting to know each other. Actually, Stella did most of the talking, for no one had ever asked her about herself and now she discovered that she liked to converse on that subject with this young man. In fact, she talked so much that she forgot where she was and remembered only at the last minute. "Oh! the time! I've got to tell mother superior you ran down the back stairs," she cried.

Franco jumped up and met himself in the tall mirror that stood by the bed — a flushed young man in a whore's bedroom. How odd that a flat mirror reflects so little of the truth, he thought.

"Hurry!" Stella said, unlatching the shuttered doors to the balcony. "This way. And be careful of the bird cages out there. Whatever you do, don't make any noise. After my last customer leaves I'll open the doors and let you in. Watch out for my doves!"

Stella shut the doors and adjusted the louvers so that Franco, out on the dark balcony, could peer in and see all that went on in the lighted room. Franco crouched among the bamboo bird cages and wondered how he could watch and not watch at the same time, for on the one hand he felt it was dishonorable to spy on the woman he loved and on the other hand he had given her his promise to spy in order to win her. He was turning this round and round in his mind when he heard the bedroom door open. He peeked between the slats and began to watch.

Well, what can I tell you? Stella's first customer was a cranky Neapolitan businessman whose limp thing wouldn't get hard no matter how she handled it, until he gave her an order to do thus and so with this and this. Next came the elegant son of a local landowner, a youth with a long nose who confused top with bottom, front with back, and one thing with another. And after him there came two Royalist officers, big men who tossed off their uniforms and shoved each other around like playful athletes before they set to work on Stella. It grew to be a very long night.

When her last customer had gone, Stella unlatched the doors to the balcony and whispered to Franco, *Come in.* He arose slowly and unsteadily from the lattice of shadows amid the bamboo bird cages. She poured two brimming glasses of brandy, drank one straight down and handed the other to him. But Franco stood wordless in the balcony doorway, his face white as a sheet of paper, his eyes dead as stones.

"Ah," Stella said gently. "I can see you've had a hard night."

Franco stared straight ahead, as if he were deaf, dumb and blind.

"I like you," she said. She looked at him, then sighed and drank down his brandy. "Actually, I love you and I'm sorry I didn't tell you before," she added.

He walked uncertainly into the room.

"Listen," she told him. "Garibaldi has landed and there's going to be a big battle tonight. You've got to get home."

"That's what I want, a good fight." He seemed to awaken.

"Did you hear me? Garibaldi has landed. When the troops find out they'll be shooting at anything that moves. You've got to get home."

"I'd like to kill a few troops myself," he said. "A few Neapolitans. Some landowners. A couple of officers." He laughed and his eyes brightened.

"Carissimo," she said, putting her hand to his cheek. "Garibaldi is immortal but you are not. Stay out of it. Go someplace safe."

But Franco had already crossed the room and now he threw open the chamber door and vaulted down the stairway, strode through a maroon parlor of gilded chairs, torn playing cards and overturned wineglasses, and burst into the street. He ran, turned away from the bordello and ran down whatever avenue opened for him, ran through a city of crumbling masonry and stucco and shuttered windows with no sound anywhere except his own clattering footfall. He ran where the streets themselves led, rushing now down a cobbled alley to a yet narrower passage that hurled him headlong into the Cathedral Square which abruptly swirled into a crackling chaos of gunfire, screams and plunging horses.

Garibaldi had landed. Everyone in Reggio had know he was coming, the only question was when. Italy is separated from Sicily by the Straits of Messina, and the northern end of the Straits is so narrow that anyone on the Italian side could climb a hill and look over the water to Garibaldi's camp and watch his men hammering together supply rafts, or inspect his make-shift flotilla of steamboats, fishing boats, rowboats and barges pulled up on the sand. The desolate King in Naples knew he was coming. He had ordered his warships to patrol the Straits, and he had packed 16,000 handsomely dressed troops into that part of Italy. The old general at the castle in Reggio certainly knew he was coming. He calculated that Garibaldi would cross the Straits and rush up from the shore to the streets of the city. That's why he positioned his colonel and the men of the 14th Line out front, had ordered them to bivouac in the large Square before the Cathedral. He figured that Garibaldi was an ordinary mortal.

On the morning of August 19 Garibaldi did appear, but not on the shore opposite his camp and not at the narrow northern end of the Straits at all, but on an empty stretch of beach thirty miles to the south. The Royal Navy never saw him. He simply appeared, materializing quietly out of the limpid dawn air with his men on a patch of sand that sloped gently up to a wilderness of cactuses and aloes. Eventually Royalist warships came up over the horizon and drew near and since not even Garibaldi could hide a steamboat on an open beach he and his crazy quilt army were discovered. The warships blew apart the grounded steamboat, but by then the entire army on the beach had vanished. Garibaldi had a simple plan. First he would march north to rendezvous with partisans already in the countryside, then he would transform all his men into substanceless shadows. The next night some would slip past the soldiers who guarded the city gates and once inside would glide noiselessly toward the Cathedral Square. He and the others would condense out of the black night air on the hills behind Reggio. When the redshirts and the Royalists were in blind battle in front of the Cathedral, Garibaldi and the rest of his army would sweep down upon the city and it would be theirs. The plan worked like a miracle. And Franco just happened to rush into the Square the moment the fight began.

✳ ✳ ✳ ✳ ✳

The morning after the battle was quiet in the bordello Conca d'Oro. Stella sat in the half-shuttered light of her room with her forgotten sewing in her lap and gazed blankly at the dirty wall. She tried not to think of Franco, because whenever she did her heart felt hollow and heavy at the same time. She sighed and wondered what the next thousand years would bring and she was trying not to think at all when there was a BOOM and one of the shutters burst into splinters above her head. It took her a moment to realize that somebody had fired a shotgun at her balcony doors. "Stella DiMare!" he cried. She jumped up and put her cheek to the margin of the shutter, peering into the narrow street below. "Stella DiMare!" Of course it was Franco standing there, a pistol in his belt and a shotgun in his hand, shouting up at her. She pressed her back against the wall. "Yes!" she cried.

"My name is Franco Morelli from the town of

29

Morano in Cosenza!" There was another BOOM as the top of the other door to the balcony exploded, filling the air with wood chips.

"I remember you," Stella shouted, her eyes shut against the soft patter of bird shot and plaster falling from the ceiling.

"Thank you," he cried. "I've come back to tell you what I saw in your room last night."

She opened her eyes. "And what did you see?"

"A jackass, a dog, and two pigs!" he shouted.

"Very clever! You're the cleverest young man I know."

"And you," he called up to her. "I saw you, diva."

Stella opened the shredded balcony shutters and stood there a moment, looking down on him. His necktie was gone, his shirt was open, his jaw was dark with a day's stubble — a handsome young man. She said nothing. Her face was as calm as the sea when night is over and morning about to begin and her eyes shimmered with sadness.

"Oh, yes. Everyone looked at you but I'm the only one who saw you. I know you for what you are. Diva. Goddess. I keep trying but I haven't shot anybody yet," he cried. "Will you marry me!"

Stella looked into Franco's face and smiled, then she turned and unlatched the door to one of the bamboo cages and withdrew one dove and another. She tossed them into the air where they blossomed in a flurry of white wings, then beat their way in a soaring helical sweep skyward, circle upon circle, one following the other like melody in a round. She smiled because she loved Franco. Now she flung open the other cages and as the doves shot up around her like rockets she leaned over the rail to say, "Yes, I will marry you." But by then the street was empty and Franco gone.

Franco had run off before Stella had answered, because he was afraid she might say no. In all other ways he was brave. The next day he hiked out of the city and up the hills northward, climbing to join the Garibaldini camped on the slopes high above the Straits. Franco chose a patch of ground slovenly with broken mud banks, cactuses, tangled vineyards and orchards, chose it because the view was splendid. Below him on the lower terraces of the mountain were the Royalist troops, and way down below the Royalists flowed the blue waters of the Straits, and on the other side stood the lilac headlands of Sicily with smoky Mongibello (Mt. Etna) to the south and the great Tyrrhenian Sea like azure enamel to the north horizon. Franco sat back against a crooked olive tree, his shotgun across his knees, but the call to advance and fire never came. Instead, the men of both armies — the redshirts in the balcony, the Royalists in the lower tiers — watched an artillery duel between the distant cannoneers on the Sicilian point and the warships of the Royal Navy. The following day Garibaldi gave the order to advance without firing. The men stood up, stretched and began to descend, step by step, upon the Royalist troops. Franco couldn't believe what was happening. Now and again cotton puffs of smoke appeared below and cannonballs shrieked up at them, thudding into the mountainside, and every so often he heard the crack of enemy rifle fire, but everyone continued to step carefully downward with their weapons silent. At one point word was passed along that they were to halt, so they halted. Franco sat on the ground and stared glumly at the town below, knowing that if the fight continued in this fashion he would never get to shoot anybody. Then he saw Garibaldi close at hand on the brown hillside where he stood talking with three of his officers. He had a full golden beard, wore a loose red shirt stained with sweat and he carried a long sword, was using it just now to make a sweeping orchestral gesture toward the gray mountains further north. Two of the men broke off and headed up the hill while Garibaldi and the remaining officer began to walk down toward the enemy. His voice was strange, more like music than speech, and Franco remembered it for the rest of his life. Word came again to advance without firing, so they did, and in a little while the King's soldiers threw down their rifles and surrendered. In a few days Garibaldi was to gallop north to Naples, disarming and sending home ten thousand Royalist troops on the way, and when he rode through the mountain provinces of Calabria, Basilicata and Campania, men would come forward to touch his hand, women would hold babies aloft to receive his blessing, and he was greeted as a god.

Now Franco trudged down the last hillock, crossed a dirt road and walked onto the empty shore. He broke open his shotgun, unloaded his pistol and laid them on the dry pebbles. Nearer the water he saw something like a discarded banner lying on the sand and when he looked more closely he saw that it was a forgotten pile of laundry, a woman's white dress and blue robe folded loosely and anchored there by the handful of sea shells heaped upon it. He tried not to think of Stella, but everything reminded him of her. He sighed. He pulled off his shoes, threw off his shirt and waded into the water. He washed his face, his scorched neck, his arms. The scent of brine and lemon blossoms, the swaying of the sea anemones, the convoluted drifting braids of tawny seaweed— everything reminded him of Stella. He gazed at the waves that came forever forward to meet him, waves that still rise and curl and, curling, fall like scalloped shells upon that beach, and as he watched a wave broke into foam and it was Stella who stood before him, wringing the seawater from her hair while she waded ashore. "Franco," she called to him. "You are a rationalist, a freethinker and a mathematician and I am the goddess who says yes." They had many children, each one as beautiful as her mother.

4

WE KNOW THESE THINGS because a grandson of Angelo Cavallù married a granddaughter of Stella DiMare on the dock in Boston in 1904, and the stories were passed down from one generation to another. Angelo, half man and half stallion, loved to tell the story of his wedding night, and his son Fimi told it to his own son Pacifico and Pacifico, who married on the dock in Boston in 1904, used to tell it at his big Sunday dinners where his children heard it and they, in turn, told it to their children. As for the story of Stella DiMare, a woman so beautiful her looks could stun, Stella refused to be ashamed and told all her children — seven daughters — the true story of how she had met their father in the bordello Conca d'Oro. Her daughter Diva told it with sympathy and amusement to her own daughter Marianna but Marianna, who married Pacifico on the dock in Boston in 1904, could never be coaxed to tell it at their big Sunday dinners, or only rarely and only if the children had left the table, for she had told them a different version. It was a very nice version, but not true.

These stories were first written down by Nick Pellegrino. His mother Marissa was one of Pacifico Cavallù's daughters, but Nick didn't hear them from her. His mother didn't know what to make of a great-grandfather who was part horse or a great-grandmother who worked in a house of prostitution, and she was too embarrassed to tell such tales to her son. As it happened, Nick heard them from his aunt Regina (Gina) who was one of his mother's sisters. When Gina was a girl she was told that Stella Di-Mare was a singer with the voice of an angel, that the Conca d'Oro was an opera house and what Franco witnessed that night was a production of Verdi's *La Traviata*, the opera about a Parisian courtesan. As I said, a very nice version. But the facts about the Conca d'Oro got passed along from older sister to younger and the true story always came out.

As I said, Nick wrote down these tales and we should all be grateful for that, but he got certain things wrong — like names, dates, generations, and that fable about getting married on the dock. Of course, when he heard these tales from his aunt he was twenty-two, she was thirty-two, and they were both lying naked on her sunny bed after making love, so he may have been too unfocused to remember much. Gina was the youngest of all his aunts. Gina's mother, Marianna Cavallù, had nine children – first came four girls, then four boys, and only then came Gina. She was as beautiful as her sisters and as wild as her brothers, so ungovernable that she ran away from her mother, or was sent off by her father, to live with one of her older married sisters, the thought being that her older sister would be better able to control her. That sister was Nick's mother, and Nick always said he had a crush on Gina since he was five years old. By the time Nick was twenty-two, Gina was a restless widow, her husband having been lost at sea in World War II. After the war Gina owned a café in the fishing town of Gloucester, on Cape Ann, in Massachusetts. That's where this happened in the summer of 1952.

So there's Nick in white trousers and a sky-blue open shirt, a handsome kid with scratchy stubble on his jaws. And there's Gina with bare arms and a tight white jersey with a dab of shadow beneath each nipple. He grabs her breast, gives her a kiss on the mouth, and she slaps his face hard — *whack! whack!* — this way and that. *"Four years at college and you've learned absolutely nothing!"* she cries, her eyes brimming with tears. He came back later with his arms full of flowers and over the next few days one thing led to another, as it will. Gina liked to talk after making love, liked to loaf on the bed and gossip about anything at all. She would lean back against the heaped pillows, the wisps of hair in her armpits damp and curled, a valley of sweat glistening between her breasts. And in the faint warm aroma of fresh dough that rose from her flesh after strenuous love making, she would light a cigarette and take the clam shell ashtray from the bed table and place it on her stomach, right over her deep sweat-filled belly button. "You have beautiful legs," she told Nick one day. "You inherited those legs from your great, great grandfather. Did you know that? Stop fidgeting and let me tell you something." That's how he first heard those stories.

Their love making was their special secret and they never guessed that everyone in the family soon sensed that something was going on. Gina's brothers figured that Gina and Nick were banging each other and it might be illegal or revolting or only very foolish, but there it was and somebody should break them up before anyone else found out. Gina's sisters felt she was overly fond of Nick, maybe way too fond, but that was only because he was he was young and so full of life, and because after Gina had learned how her husband had been swept from the deck of his Coast Guard ship she had gone crazy and her heart had frozen. Now her heart had thawed and that was all to the good, but somebody should break them up before it went too far. Nick's mother seemed to be the only one who believed that Nick, whom she still thought of as a rather sensitive boy, merely had a crush on Gina. Nick's father asked Gina's brother Mercurio, the brother closest to Nick in age, to drive down to Gloucester. "Don't bawl out Gina," he told Mercurio. "But when you have Nick alone, talk to him — don't ask what's going on, don't ever talk about that. Just remind him he's finished school, he's grown up, and now he has to get serious. When the subject gets around to women, tell him you don't like men who take advantage of women, younger or older. That will start him thinking. He won't listen to me, because I'm his father and he thinks I don't know anything about —" Here he broke off and searched for the right words. "Women and romance.

But he'll listen to you," he said.

So Mercurio drove down to Gloucester in his red sports car, spent a night with Nick driving from one roadhouse to another, and the romance between Gina and Nick came to end. And Gina's sisters were right: Gina's heart had thawed. She no longer thought of her husband being swept into the black Atlantic, no longer heard him shouting in the icy water while the ship vanished behind a mountainous wave, no longer watched while he thrashed and bobbed and froze to death. Many years later – the soft summer of 1985 – at the double wedding where Gina married Marshfield Thomas and Gina's granddaughter Aurora married Jens, Nick learned from Mercurio that the whole family had known something was going on between Nick and Gina back in 1952, and Nick's father had sent Mercurio to Gloucester to bring it to an end.

5

NOW LET ME GO BACK AND PICK UP the loose end of that earlier story, the one about Angelo Cavallù and Ava, and continue from there. Angelo and Ava Cavallù named their first child Giuseppe Calatafimi Cavallù — named him Giuseppe (Joseph), not after Italy's patron saint, Joseph, minimus husband of Mary, mother of Jesus, but for the great Giuseppe Garibaldi, and named him Calatafimi for the place where Garibaldi and Angelo and the other Red Shirts had fought their way up a hillside to blow away the Royalist army. This Giuseppe Calatafimi was called plain Fimi. He was born with thighs and legs like a horse, but not so emphatically as his father, and now at eighteen he was already a hand taller than the older man. Young Fimi wasn't a scholar, it's true, but he did know two short prayers by heart, had his multiplication tables up to nine times nine, could do long division, and though he barely knew how to read he could sign his name with a handsome flourish. Furthermore, he was like a young god with animals, could calm a spooked horse by sheer talk, call goats and pigs and bulls to his side, or whistle a bird so it ate from his hand, and about a year ago he had discovered he could do much the same with young women — farm girls, house maids, serving girls in taverns.

One night in the spring of 1879 Fimi couldn't fall asleep. He felt thirsty, or perhaps hungry, he couldn't tell which, or maybe he was getting light-headed with the scent of lemon blossoms from the neighbor's orchards, or possibly it was his legs which were growing tense with compressed energy. He got up and pulled on his pants, careful not to wake his brother. He crept down the hall past his sisters' bedroom, groped down the back stairway to the kitchen and across the cool stone floor to the dirt courtyard, then ran across the courtyard, leapt the back gate, and galloped out to the field. Pieces of the moon flickered on the stream which separated the Cavallù land from the neighbor's orchards. He sat low on the gravel bank and the cool touch of the water on his feet and ankles soothed him. The stars looked hazy and he wondered if the scent of lemon blossoms had thickened the air. He was getting drowsy when a patch of night from the shadowy orchard came splashing across the stream to slip past him. Or it would have slipped past if he hadn't stood up. "Hey!" he whispered. "Who are *you*?" he said.

The person stopped as still as a stone. "No one," she said at last.

"You must be someone," Fimi said, walking over to get a better look. "I've seen you before. You work for the Baldos," he said.

"So?"

"What are you doing over here?"

"Nothing."

"Where are you going in the middle of the night?"

"Palermo."

"Ah! You're the girl the DiSecco woman bought. How do you like being a lady's maid?"

"Work is work. It's the school part I can't stand."

Fimi laughed. "You'll get a good husband out of it. That's the deal, isn't it?"

"I don't plan to get married to some old *contadino* with cow shit on his boots. I'd rather die in Palermo than live out here."

"You have a long walk ahead of you. Why don't you —"

"If you come a step closer I'll crack your nuts!"

Fimi laughed. "Tough city girl. Take it easy. Sit down and we'll talk. Only talk. It's a good night for talk."

But she had already turned and was walking into the dark field.

"By the way," he said. "If you're looking for the road to Palermo, it's down the slope, not over where you're headed."

"You're lying," she said, hesitating.

"Don't get lost. —Look at the moon. It's only a slice. Wait a few days, there'll be more moon and you'll be able to see where you're going. And you never know who's sleeping in those fields."

She glanced at the moon, then came back and sat on a stone somewhat above him, out of his reach. "I still think you're lying," she muttered. As a matter of fact, he was. She hadn't lived in the country long enough to know which way the moon grew and to-morrow night it would be even thinner. Fimi asked her name. Cinderella, she said tartly. And I'm prince Cavallù, he countered. He reached for her foot and she swung it out of reach. "Come on. What are you afraid of?" he asked her.

"They say you're animals."

"Who says?"

"Everybody. Signora DiSecco and her brother."

"No one would call DiSecco or her brother Baldo animals. We think of them as vegetables."

"And I know about the vendetta between Signor Baldo and your father," she said.

Fimi laughed. "There's no vendetta — maybe one of our sheep strayed onto Baldo's land and came home to us naked, so a few days later a barrel of Baldo's lemons suddenly turned rotten, then one of our goats got shot, then a few of their trees got chopped down. That's all. No vendetta," he assured her. "My father and Signor Baldo get along like brothers."

Fimi had edged up beside her; she watched him closely from the corner of her eyes, but she didn't move.

"What do you do for the signora?" he asked, simply to keep her talking.

"I prepare her bath every morning, light her bed-room lamps every night, and do everything else in between. Whatever she wants."

Fimi murmured sympathetically, brushed her cheek with his hand and she snapped at him, biting his little finger almost in two.

44

"Aiiii! —You work a long hard day," he said when he could, sucking the blood from his finger. "She beat you much?" He took a rag from his pocket and wrapped it around the finger.

"No. If she gets angry she locks me in my room with a book and won't let me out until I've copied a whole page, word for word. But she's all right, mostly all right. Sometimes she'll give me one of her old dresses to keep and she even leaves the beads on it. Like this one," she said, smoothing the fabric over her knees. "She gave me this. It's very nice, isn't it?"

"It's very black. I can hardly see where you leave off and the night air begins."

"She wears black, only black, for her dead husband. "

Fimi's fingertips brushed her shoulder just an instant. "Ah, that's you," he said. "In the dark I couldn't tell. You were going to say something about the terrible work."

"The work isn't terrible," she told him.

"Then why are you running away?"

"It's like being in school!" she said irritably. "She tells me, Don't use that word, it's vulgar, and don't stand like that, don't show so much skin, don't use that word again, say this word, wash your hair like this so it shines. —Then I have to sit on a stool while she stands behind me and brushes my hair. She says, You can call me Signora Sofia when there's just us two. —She loves to brush my hair."

"Of course she does," Fimi said.

"All day the house is quiet as a tomb and at night

everybody sleeps. What else is there to do out here? And they're too old to do anything anyway. Signor Baldo is old, his man is old, the cook is ancient, both maids are antiques, the overseer is decrepit, the watchdog is blind. I never see a living person —" Abruptly she stopped talking because Fimi had stroked her hair gently, just once. Now there was only the sound of the water rippling around the rocks in the stream. Fimi stroked again and she resumed talking. "They've divided the house, so Signora DiSecco has half and her brother has half. Signora has a room with nothing in it but books and that's where she reads and the only noise is scritch-scritch-scritch when she writes. Signor Baldo has a room, too, but not so big as hers, where he keeps his ledgers and his guns — he's very proud of his guns — and that's where he writes down the number of every little thing he owns, how much of this, how many of that, how much it costs and how much it sells for."

"They're very strange people, both of them," Fimi agreed, laying back in the long grass. "The stars look bigger tonight. And they look wet. Look. Lie back," he said, putting a warm hand on her arm. As soon as the girl lay beside him he rolled onto his elbow to face her, waiting while she talked ever more rapidly about DiSecco and Baldo, how they sat at opposite ends of the long dinner table and argued about everything and when you heard them stop it meant that Signor Baldo had shaken open his newspaper and his sister had turned to her book. Fimi brushed her forehead with his lips, kissed her cheek, her mouth. During the next half hour one caress led to another until Fimi's Cinderella abruptly shook him aside. "Jesus," she panted. "Jesus Christ! I've got to go. If Signora DiSecco finds I'm gone she'll lock me in my room and won't let me out till I've copied a whole damn book." She threw herself on Fimi, saying, "You'd better be here tomorrow night," and bit his earlobe, then leaped up and *splash-splash* vanished into the dark.

Now, to be fair, I have to say something about Signora Sonia DiSecco. At eighteen Sonia had married Major DiSecco, a handsome reckless spendthrift who was killed four years later, ambushed with his entire troop by the brigands he had been pursuing. Sonia, stunned with grief, returned to the Baldo villa to live with her unmarried brother. Her grief receded but something in her remained awry, broken or missing. As a school girl Sonia had admired the British for aiding the Italians against the Bourbon Royalists during the Risorgimento, but now her admiration grew to a passion that embraced all things British — Parliament, Shakespeare, beef, tea, the adversarial judicial system, Isaac Newton's calculus, the poetry of Percy Bysshe Shelley, and on and on. She had never heard English spoken, but had taught herself how to read it and had recently begun a translation into Sicilian of Mary Wollstonecraft's *A Vindication of the Rights of Women.* She believed ardently that education ennobled people and was exhilarated when compulsory two-year primary school was legislated in 1877 — now everyone would have to complete second grade! And since we're talking about Sonia, I must add that she had not *bought* her maid in Palermo. The girl's parents had many more children than they could care for, so Sonia alleviated their poverty with a little cash and took the girl in as a helper and ward, all with the understanding that Sonia would educate her and find her a suitable husband. True, usually it was a poor girl from the country who was brought in to the city this way, but Signora DiSecco was never conventional.

Fimi waited by the stream the next night, but she didn't come, nor the following night when the moon was pared down even more. He decided to go to Signor Baldo's to find her, to see her even if only from a distance — and he wanted to make his exploration look innocent. So in the middle of the morning, while everyone was busy doing one thing or another, Fimi led his favorite horse — a spirited mare, glossy as a chestnut — led her without a bridle or saddle, walked her across the field by the hank of her mane in his fist, splashed across the stream and into the lemon orchard and broke out the other side. There he let go of her mane, whacked her rump and ran behind her, shouting and whistling as if trying to catch her, driving her toward the back of Villa Baldo whose new roof tiles loomed over the greenery just ahead. The mare burst through the screen of aloe bushes pursued by Fimi who chased her past the row of bee hives, past the doorway where the dog lay sleeping and the stucco wall and the grape arbor under the second-floor windows, then around the well and through a clutter of clucking hens, back to the bee hives and around again. Signor Baldo had popped up at a window at this end and — Ah, ha! — the girl was at a window at the other end, her arm cradling some books. Fimi stopped running, pulled off his shirt and as the mare came around the well he began flapping his shirt at her, whistling, shouting *Ai! Ai! Ai!* while memorizing the second-floor window where his Cinderella stood. When he had completed the survey, Fimi grabbed the mare's mane, brought her to a halt and came in a running leap to mount her. He was out of breath, his naked chest heaving and glistening with sweat, but he laughed he was so happy. Only after he had whipped his horse with his shirt and was cantering away did he see Signora DiSecco standing in the dappled shade of the grape arbor, pen in hand, watching him.

The moon was only a sliver that night and the sky thick with stars when Fimi crept into the Villa Baldo grape arbor, clambered up a post, pulled himself through a mat of vines and crawled along a thick vine-tangled beam toward the casement window which looked like a black mirror. He tapped on the glass, waited a few moments. He put his nose to the glass and peered in, saw nothing at first and then — ah! He drew back and the casement swung out with a hushed scraping sound. He swung his legs over the sill and dropped into the room. Fimi heard the rustle of falling fabric, the click of beads, and turned to see the dark shimmer of starlight on her hair and a gleam of flesh. "Where —" he began to say, but already her hands were on his shirt and with half a word, or maybe not a word but a panting breath, she ripped his shirt open, the buttons snapping off pop-pop-pop, then her arm was around his neck and her full weight pulled him down to his knees, down upon her, down upon the floor.

Everyone wants details, but the story has been handed around so many times the details have rubbed off. All I can tell you is that after their hushed and half-stifled frenzy she kissed his wounded ear and panted *mio stadduni* or *picu stadduni* — my stallion or little stallion. And that's all. As for Fimi, the love-making that night was the wildest in his life, until the next night which was even wilder, and so it went night after night after night. He wanted it to go on forever, but it came to an end two weeks after it had started. It ended the day that Signora DiSecco, who rode horses the way men do, went galloping by on the road to Palermo, and half an hour later her brother rattled past in a buggy, headed to Palermo too. By evening everyone had learned that the girl Signora DiSecco had bought in the city had run away. Whether she had returned to the poor neighborhood she had come from, or whether she had gone someplace else, or had been waylaid by the men with nothing who slept in the fields, Fimi never knew, but he knew it was over.

✳ ✳ ✳ ✳ ✳

Now a few words about Signor Baldo. He wanted a wife. At the death of his father he had taken over the estate — a crumbling farmhouse, surrounded by disorderly orchards and a withered vineyard — and made it profitable. Now he was prosperous, almost forty years old and he wanted a wife. He hadn't been able to marry, he complained, because his young sister occupied half the villa and her rants upset every decent family between Trapani and Palermo. Baldo was courting a woman named Isabella (quiet, ample shape, good-size vineyard) but when Isabella's pious family were finally seated at his table his sister Sonia had lectured them on the virtues of universal literacy. Isabella's father had laughed angrily at Sonia, informing her that if her personal maid ever learned how to read there would be no privacy for Sonia or anyone else. Sonia had then become inflamed and ridiculed the pope for forbidding Catholics to vote or to run for office. It was Sonia's passionate rudeness, not her radical opinions that bothered Baldo.

In fact, he liked to confess that in his youth he had read Mazzini and had admired Francesco Crispi, the young Sicilian revolutionary who had wanted to make Italy a republic. But Mazzini was an idealist and when Crispi grew older and wiser he helped to make Italy *not* a republic but a monarchy. Twenty years had passed: now the king and his politicians were far away up North and had forgotten about Sicily, as usual. Baldo's favorite story was how when Garibaldi and his Red Shirts came ashore to liberate Sicily the first thing they did was ask for a map. "*Sicily wasn't on their maps!* You see, the Northern Italians have always felt, deep in their hearts, that Italy stops at the beach in Reggio Calabria. On the other side of the water is the Island of Sicily which to them is not quite Africa but not really Italy, either. So nothing changes here. The important thing is not politics," said Baldo. "The important thing is to work, to have children, and to hold your land from generation to generation."

One day — it must have been two or three months after the girl ran off — Baldo and his sister Sonia DiSecco arrived at Angelo Cavallù's place. Angelo stood in the wide front doorway, his hands on his hips, not knowing what to expect. He was older than when you saw him last; now he had vigorous gray hair and the physical aplomb of a sturdy Arabian horse. Baldo was dressed neither formally nor informally, but was wearing a long face and carried what looked like a polished cigar box in his hand. His sister Sofia was dressed in black, as usual, but in addition she wore a black net veil. Angelo and Baldo noded stiffly to each other; Baldo drew his sister forward, Angelo bowed to her and led them to the sitting room. *"What?"* Angelo asked him. *"Private,"* Baldo answered. Angelo turned and led them farther to his private back room — one big window, a desk, four chairs, a shelf of jumbled ledgers, papers, wine glasses, and in the corner a large oak gear from the mill, a splintered oak axel, an egg shaped stone with a groove so you could bind it to a stick to make a hammer, two bamboo fishing poles, and other such things. He brought a rush-bottom chair and placed it beside Signora DiSecco who remained standing, her back as straight as when she rode horseback. Baldo opened the box — "A gift," he said — and placed on the desk a revolver with a dark grip and a very long barrel, setting it down ever so gently, as if it might break. Angelo took it up and looked at it without expression. "Remarkable," he said politely. "How long is the barrel?"

"Nineteen centimeters, at least," said Baldo. "It's American. A Colt Single Action Army revolver. Very powerful, very reliable. Six shots. I have another just like it."

Angelo took three wine glasses from the row on the top shelf, went to wood cabinet that had a black iron key in its keyhole, pulled open the door and removed a bottle of wine. He set the three glasses on his desk beside the Colt Single Action Army revolver and filled them. He nodded to Signor Baldo to speak.

"Your son Fimi is the father of the baby now growing inside my sister Sofia," Baldo told him.

For a moment nothing happened. Angelo frowned and sank ever deeper in thought, motionless. Then, as if merely to break the lengthening silence, he handed a glass of wine to Sofia and to Baldo. Sofia lifted her veil to drink, revealing her red-rimmed eyes. Angelo drained his glass, threw open the door to the back courtyard and cried *"Fimi!"* then slammed the door shut, rattling every pane of glass in the house. About a minute later Fimi strolled into the room, closed the door behind him and looked around with his hands on his hips, clearly puzzled. Sofia cried, *"Mio stadduni!"* — my stallion! Fimi looked at her, the color vanished from his face and he crashed to the floor in a faint. Sofia dropped to her knees, cradled Fimi's head in her lap and wept. Baldo drank a bit of wine, appeared to savor the taste, then drained his glass. Angelo stood with his arms folded, looking down at the couple on the floor.

Fimi opened his eyes and scrambled to his feet and Sofia stood up, tossed her veil aside and wiped her eyes. Angelo put his hand on his son's shoulder and they went out to the hard dirt courtyard. From inside the room Baldo and Sonia watched Angelo and Fimi talking and gesturing wildly while the sun beat down like a hammer on an anvil. Finally they ceased talking and Angelo returned to the silent room where Baldo and Sonia stood exactly as before — she with black glistening eyes, he with his empty wine glass at his chest. "Donna DiSecco," said Angelo, holding the door open. "Fimi will now show you our cork tree. One hundred years old, at least." Sonia lifted her chin and walked out to Fimi who waited in the checkered shade of the distant cork oak, calm and brave, like a man about to be hanged.

Angelo refilled Baldo's glass and his own, then placed two chairs facing each other in front of the desk. They sat down. Angelo took up the Colt revolver, ran a finger along the bluish barrel, squinted into the cylinder — it was unloaded — turned the weapon this way and that in his hand, then abruptly set it down as if he had just then remembered what they were doing here. Up to now they had been speaking a mixture of Florentine Italian and Sicilian, but now they spoke only Sicilian. "You want your sister to marry an eighteen-year-old?" he asked.

"An eighteen-year-old who is the father of her baby, yes," Baldo said, clapping a hand on each knee.

"Be reasonable. There must be a different way. She's eleven years older than he is. Your sister is twenty-nine and —"

"She's just barely turned twenty-eight and your son is almost nineteen. That's scarcely nine years difference," he said, leaning forward.

"How would Fimi support a wife? And where would they live? In a mud hut like *mezzadri*?" The *mezzadri* were sharecroppers who were allowed to use the land, but only for a few years at a time so they wouldn't improve it, and they had to give most of what they produced to the land owner — an ingenious system.

Baldo leaned back and spread his arms. "You're a successful miller. He's your son. You're his father. His problems are your problems, not mine."

Angelo studied the floor at his feet for a minute, then handed Baldo his glass, took up his own, and they drank. "That jackass Major DiSecco went through your sister's dowry in six months. What could she bring to a marriage now?"

"A complete library," Baldo said. "Much of it in English."

Angelo smiled, showing all his large square teeth.

"Many of the books have fine bindings," Baldo continued. "Including a couple illustrated with geometric diagrams, the pages written in a pagan language, maybe Moorish, from the old days. I hate to think of giving up all those books. The room will be bare and hollow without them. But she loves her library." He sighed with regret for the loss of those books, then drained his glass and set it gently on the desk.

"She also loves that straw-colored wine you press from the little vineyard — a hectare, I think — on the road to Alcamo. I'm sure she'd enjoy sharing that patch of grapes with her young husband."

"That's four hectares and it's the only vineyard

I have! I can't give that up." Baldo shook his head. "That little patch of grapes would seal the marriage," Angelo said with finality. He drained his glass and set it on the desk so hard it rang. "Your sister will no longer command half your villa! You'll be able to entertain decent families and their chaste, fertile daughters, one of whom who has a vineyard of twenty-five hectares waiting for her."

Angelo sat back in his chair, folded his arms and watched Baldo. Baldo, who sat with his hands capped over his knees, looked somberly at the floor a while, then looked up speculatively past Angelo at the ceiling even longer, then looked at Angelo.

Sonia Baldo DiSecco, widow of that jackass Major DiSecco, and young Giuseppe Calatafimi Cavallù, called Fimi, were married July 30, 1879. Their child was born sometime in March, or maybe earlier as some say, in 1880, a remarkably large sturdy infant, and was named Pacifico (Peaceful) to embody the peace and reconciliation of the two neighboring families. It was an interesting marriage.

6

S IGNOR BALDO INTENDED AN INSULT when he
said that the Cavallù family were animals, or
that the males, anyway, were animals, or were
at least half horse — or whatever it was he said.
Baldo was one of those conservatives who strove to
keep up the old social distinctions between men and
beasts, but many Sicilians didn't see things that way.
The people who managed large estates rarely made a
difference between the work animals and the work-
men on their land — they cursed them, beat and
fed them the same, housed them the same — and,
frankly, the poor saw no distinction between bosses
and beasts. Society was fluid that way. As for Signora Sonia Baldo DiSecco Cavallù, she loved her
young stallion, her *stadduni*, and in the frenzy of love
making would drum her heels against Fimi's hard
hindquarters, spurring him on.

Ordinary Sicilians lived close to their animals. In
country towns many of the dwellings were made of
stones covered with painted stucco and these houses,
typically huddled together on steep hillsides, would
have two floors, so the cows and goats were brought
in below and the Christians lived above; that way it
was warmer in winter, too. Poorer families had only
one floor and they bedded down along side maybe

just one skinny cow or sick pig and maybe things happened that no one talked about.

Calogero Zitellone (Zitti), who married Angelo Cavallù's great granddaughter in Massachusetts, believed that the story about the half-stallion ancestor depicted the same kind of metamorphosis that Ovid wrote about. "These things happened when the world was new and was just beginning to take shape," he said. "They're true stories, but so distant in time that you have to interpret them to reveal the truth." Nicolo Pellegrino, father of Nick who wrote down those first two tales, raised his eyebrows. "You think somebody mated with a horse?"

"I was talking about metamorphoses, changes brought about by the interference of the gods — or, as you would say, genetics."

"Human's don't mate with animals," Pellegrino said.

Zitti gave a short, derisive laugh. "Never?" he said.

After the slightest hesitation, Pellegrino said, "Not successfully. If a human mates with a horse you don't get anything or you get a monstrosity."

"Sometimes you get a monstrosity and sometimes you don't," Zitti said. "These ancient stories are true, but nowadays people don't believe what they don't see. There's hardly a horse in Boston anymore, and no cows. There'll come a day when people will have gotten so far from horses and cows they won't believe they ever existed. They won't know a horse turd from a cow flap, and that's true ignorance."

Zitti (philosopher, philologist, inventor of an onomatopoetic language) and Nicolo Pellegrino (aeronautical engineer, balloonist) were academics who relished disagreement, and that conversation took place in 1935 in Lexington, Massachusetts, in Pacifico Cavallù's green back yard as the two men walked down the bocce court, retrieved the balls and got set for another throw.

Signor Baldo was right when he said nothing much changed in Sicily, not even after the glorious Risorgimento. Garibaldi was disregarded and the idealistic Mazzini, elected to parliament, wasn't allowed to take his seat. In 1866 groups of armed men began to march toward Palermo again. The revolutionary gangs were made up of clerics, mafiosi, some local princes, angry young men looking for a fight, stray followers of Mazzini and some nostalgic Bourbon crackpots hoping to restore the old Royalists. Angelo Cavallù stayed home and repaired his mill. In Palermo the revolutionaries managed to burn police records and land leases, which was all to the good, then the Italian navy sailed in, lobbed a few shells into the city, and 40,000 Italian troops took over. European maps printed after 1870 show the Italian peninsula and Sicily all one color, because the old kingdoms and dukedoms, and even the part around Rome previously ruled by the pope, all had been put together like a grand geographic jigsaw puzzle. But neither the Italians nor the Sicilians believed in a monochromatic map and no one threw away the old flags.

7

STELLA DiMARE (WOMAN OR GODDESS — either way, her looks could knock you over) and Franco (mathematician and free thinker) were married in 1860 in Reggio Calabria. We don't know how many children they had, only that each one was as beautiful as her mother, and that the first was named Diva and the second, Morgana. Diva, born in 1861, married a fisherman named Remo Moretti in 1881 and the couple settled in a seaside town west of Palermo. The following year Diva's unmarried sister, Morgana, visited her and the next month, early in May, Morgan went to Palermo. This is what happened there.

Morgana was in the kitchen, in back, that night (May 11, 1882) when the police broke into the front room where the men were meeting. Morgana, hearing shouts, the thud of fists and the tumble and crack of furniture, jumped on a chair, stepped onto the kitchen table, reached up and pushed open the skylight and pulled herself onto the roof. She pressed the skylight shut and crouched there, her heart pounding so hard she could barely breath. As she peered into the kitchen one of the police thugs entered and swept the coffee pot and the neatly arranged cups from the table to smash on the floor.

Then he went to a shelf, took one dish at a time and hurled it at the floor or the wall, while with his other hand he held off old Signora Felice who continued to flail and grab at his throwing arm, shouting curses all the while. Morgana backed away, then stood up to look around, and little by little her trembling ceased. She could see beyond the uneven terrain of roofs to the black waters of the harbor and, way off, the dark bulk of Monte Pellegrino. She crept across the flat roof, climbed over a low wall that separated this building from its neighbor, and then continued across the next roof.

Orlando Vela, a young school teacher who also wrote newspaper articles and poetry, was in Palermo too. That same night (May 11, 1882) he was on a balcony in an unbuttoned shirt, pulling on his socks, jamming his feet into his shoes, and even before he was finished he heard voices from the bedroom — a grumpy baritone, a mollifying soprano. He climbed over the balcony rail and twisted around so he was perched there, clinging to the rail while facing the double doors which were now bounded with narrow yellow line of lamplight. He glanced down and saw a twenty foot drop to the paving stones, then looked up to find the margin of the roof only a few feet above his head. Orlando edged sideways closer to the building, steadied himself with a hand on an iron lamp bracket, climbed onto the balcony rail and hauled himself up on to the roof. The moon was half full, the sky lightly sprinkled with stars, and Orlando felt such exhilaration that he almost laughed. He felt like singing as strolled across the roof and lowered himself gently onto another that was a criss-cross of clothes lines and damp laundry.

Morgana and Orlando were making their away across this same roof, ducking around pale sheets and shadowy garments, when they bumped into each other.

"Good God!" Orlando said.

"Back off or I'll kill you!" Morgana said in a harsh whisper.

"Hey, take it easy, take it easy!" he whispered. "What have you got there? A pen? You're going to kill me with a steel nib pen?"

"Try me, I'll blind you."

Orlando laughed, Morgana lunged at him and he caught her, had his arms around her like a hoop.

"What's *wrong* with you?" he whispered, his mouth at her ear. His sense of decorum made him release her, but he still kept her wrist in his fist and was holding her at arms length, hoping she'd drop the pen, but she continued to twist and kick in furious silence until he let go. "Are you crazy? What did I ever do to you?"

"Nothing and don't try." She was panting and held the pen underhand, like a knife pointed at him, while she massaged her wrist with her other hand.

"Who are you?" he asked.

"You don't need to know. Just get out of my way."

"You sound Calabrian. You don't come from around here."

Morgana said nothing.

"Excuse me, signorina." Orlando bowed ever so slightly "Please allow me introduce myself. I'm Orlando Vela, the poet. I also write articles encouraging the spread of telegraphy, the building of paved highways and the completion of the railroad. And I teach school," he added as an afterthought.

"Railroads? It took five years to lay five miles of track. Then ten more years to lay the next ten miles! You still can't get from Messina to Palermo in a straight line." Morgana had relaxed somewhat and now she dropped the pen into the folded sheaf of papers that filled her pocket. "Because until you change the social system and control the power of the land owners and the so-called notables, you can't make progress in anything," she concluded.

"Are you some kind of female railroad engineer?"

"Are you some kind of police spy?"

"Do I look like a police spy?" he asked.

"You look like a boy who got dressed in a hurry. Your shirt's buttoned wrong, your collar has popped out. I won't disgrace myself speculating on what you've been up to. I'm sure it's not poetry or journalism or teaching, not at this hour."

"And who are you running away from? A boorish husband? It's usually a boorish husband. But in your case, I suppose not. You have no husband. Police spies? Yes, that's possible."

"Clever signor Vela."

"You're the secretary for a revolutionary group," he said, rebuttoning his shirt.

"There's no revolutionary group. Only a dozen

people who gathered to listen to a talk by a French socialist. I took notes for the committee — the group, I mean.

"You must have been the only woman there." Orlando tucked his shirt into his trousers and smoothed out the wrinkles.

"In every revolutionary movement, in every progressive period, you'll find women there," Morgana said. "The police broke up the meeting. I don't know what happened to the others."

"I'm glad you got out."

"I'd gone to the kitchen to get coffee for the men. While the fighting was going on in the front room I got away," she said.

Orlando smiled. "In every revolutionary movement, in every progressive period, women will be sent to make coffee for the men."

"You should put that cleverness to better use, signor Vela."

"Signorina, I'm at your service." He put his hand over his heart and extended his arm in an operatic gesture.

"Fine. How do we get off this roof? I can't go back the way I came."

"Neither can I."

They walked quietly to the end of the aisle of laundry, then patrolled the edge of the roof, searching for a way down, and discovered a terrace about eight feet below. "If you permit me," said Orlando, "I can hold your hands and lower you until there's only a short distance more to go, then you could drop down and not get hurt."

"I can lower myself down," Morgana told him.

"Excellent. By the way, when you drop onto that terrace everybody in the house is going to wake up."

"I'll get off before anyone comes. It's a short drop from the terrace to the street," she said.

"Where will you go?"

"That's not your concern," she said.

"I suggest we can stay here until dawn, then we can leave. Because, you know, it's not a good idea to be on the street in Palermo when it's still dark, not even for a brave socialist revolutionary."

"I should have stuck you with my pen," Morgana said. So they stayed on the roof and continued to talk in whispers, though to be exact, Orlando did most of the talking and mostly about a long poem which he was writing about Daedalus and Icarus, father and son, who made wings of sea gull feathers and flew to Sicily. He was writing it *not* in Italian, he said proudly, but in Sicilian. Eventually the sky lightened and they were able to see each other more clearly, this slender but sturdy young woman with the remarkably clear eyes, and this young man with his playful smile and rather boyish pink cheeks, now darkened with overnight stubble, like sandpaper. As they got ready to descend, Orland said, "Please allow me to accompany you and no one will bother you."

After a moment Morgana said, "Thank you, Signor Vela."

"If you tell me your name, I can pretend you're a cousin from Calabria. But I have to know your name, Signorina."

"Morgana."

"A beautiful name, a name with poetry in it. Later I'll tell you the story of Morgana the sorceress who created the —"

Morgana cut in, saying, "I know the story."

"Fine. This morning you can be Morgana Vela, my cousin, my father's brother's daughter."

"We'll need another story when we get to my sister's house. We can discuss that later. I'm sure I can come up with some good ideas."

8

ORGANA'S OLDER SISTER, you recall, was named Diva and she was married to Remo Moretti and they lived in a harbor town west of Palermo. Diva and Remo had children, among them a daughter named Marianna. Now one day in the summer of 1901 this young Marianna Moretti brought her family's bread to the *furnu*. The *furnu* was a bake house on the edge of town, a place with a large brick and stone oven where you brought your uncooked loaves to have them baked. Whenever Diva made a batch of bread dough, she would knead it and roll it and fold it into good round loaves, then put the loaves in a basket, cover them with cloth, and give them to her daughter Marianna to carry to the *furnu*. This day the baker, Grasso, was being visited by his friend Pacifico Cavallù. They had been in the army together, had been stationed in Naples, and together had visited cities even further north, and had got acquainted with different places, different people and different ways of doing things.

Now the sun was hot, so hot it was cooking the figs on the trees, and inside the *furnu* was even hotter, so here they are outside, their chairs tilted back against the broad trunk of a chestnut tree, having a lazy debate about women. "As you go south, the women get darker and more sensual," Grasso said. "My brother-in-law was with the army in Africa and he tells me that Ethiopian women actually crave sex. I noticed up north, where they sun isn't so strong, the women have lighter skin and lighter hair, like in Venice and Milan, and they get temperamentally colder, less sensual. Sicilian women are by nature sensual, but they lie about it and pretend they have no interest in sex. You have to release it in them. You can't do that with a woman from northern Europe. They're essentially frigid."

"Are you serious? All the women in Sweden are pale and blond, but they can't all be frigid," Pacifico said. "Otherwise they'd be no Scandinavians,"

"I'm speaking in general. In general, northern women are not as sensual as Mediterranean women."

"Northern women are more elegant."

Grasso thought about that a while. "In a way, yes. But I prefer sensuality. — What kind of women do you think you'd fined in North America?"

"Women from Palermo, women from Naples, women from Rome, from Torino," Pacifico said. "You can find them all there."

Grasso laughed. "I don't need to go to America to find those women." Then they debated how much money you might need before you could afford to marry a decent Sicilian woman, and that led to talk about the great Sicilian problem which is poverty and rebellion, poverty because no job pays enough and rebellion because landowners pay no taxes on land while poor people have to pay a tax on flour or they starve.

"Nobody ever starved in America," Pacifico announced.

"Here we go again. You really believe that?"

"It's true."

"Are they giving away bread in America?" Grasso asked. "Because the day when nobody starves is the day they give away bread. If you have rich people and poor people, sooner or later somebody poor is going to starve."

Pacifico laughed. "You should write a book on economics."

"You're the one who wants to get rich. I'm interested only in earning an honest living."

"Earning an honest living isn't so easy," Pacifico said. "Not in Sicily. In fact, it may be impossible."

They talked about the land owners who proclaimed that there was no poverty and the way to get rid of the Sicilian problem was to abolish compulsory education. Grasso went inside to check on some loaves and came out a few minutes later, mopping his face with a cloth. A young woman with a parasol showed up in the distance — that was Marianna, of course — walking toward them in a steady but unhurried pace, a little girl by her side.

"You're serious about leaving?" Grasso said.

"Everybody's leaving," Pacifico said. "Except the government and the mafia," he added. He gazed in meditative silence across the dirt road to the distant terracotta hills. "Because it's the same thing. They call it mafia at the bottom and government at the top. But it's all the same."

"Death and taxes," Grasso said.

"What about death and taxes?"

"God created death to punish Adam and Eve for disobeying him when they ate the fruit from the tree in the garden. Right?"

"That's the way the story goes," said Pacifico.

"I think God invented taxes at the same time."

Marianna's back was as straight as the back of a woman carrying a jug of water on her head, but she walked with the basket of unbaked loaves on her arm and in her other hand an upraised blue parasol with a fancy lace fringe. Her sister was carrying a book and kicking a stone ahead of her as she walked. Marianna was eighteen and wearing what had been a loose sea-green summer shift, but since it had been cut and sewn three years ago it was no longer loose.

"They don't have so many taxes in America," Pacifico said.

"They're socialists?"

"Capitalists."

Grasso and Pacifico stood up and Grasso greeted the young woman. When the baker and Marianna, plus her little sister, went into the bake house, Pacifico decided to stay in the cool shade of the chestnut tree, then abruptly followed them and got entangled in the swaying curtain of beads in the doorway. The baker took Marianna's loaves and put them in a big flat pan along side other unbaked loaves which were waiting their turn to go into the oven. The only way you could tell your bread from anyone else's was by the way you had marked your loaves — by cut-

74

ting an initial or some other zigzag into the dough crust — so Marianna glanced at the other loaves and scratched a quick M on each of hers. "You have beautiful penmanship, young lady," said Pacifico. Marianna looked at him a moment, then laughed and said, "I know how to write, sir, if that's what you mean."

"What happens if you take home someone else's loaf?" he asked, just to prolong the conversation.

"I wouldn't do that."

"You might do it by mistake and not even know you were doing it," he told her.

"Then I'd bring it back," she said, turning to leave, her hand on her little sister's head.

"But what if you ate it before you discovered it belonged to somebody else?" He spoke hurriedly because she was already at the door. "That would be stealing and stealing's a sin," he said in a rush.

"There'd be no sin if I gave my own in exchange for it," Marianna said over her shoulder.

They went out and Pacifico, trailing behind her, was caught again in the beaded strands swaying in the doorway.

He got outside and, at a loss for something to engage the young woman, he turned to her young sister. "What's the name of your book?" he asked her.

"That's mine, sir," Marianna told him. "She doesn't read things like that yet." She took the book from her sister and put it in the basket under the cloth.

"Ah. Well. Now you've put the book to bed," Pacifico said. "I'll never know what it is."

Marianna laughed. Pacifico was twenty-one, wearing a white collarless shirt, and he had fledgling beard on his chin and jaws — a stranger, an interesting man, handsome. He looked about to speak and even started to open his mouth, but said nothing, so to help him out she said, "If you're interested, it's called *The Lady of the Camellias* and it's by Alexandre Dumas, the son. He's a well known French author, famous for his novels," she said with school-girl pedantry, "But this is a translation. Because I don't know how to read French. It's the book Giuseppe Verdi made into *La Traviata*."

"A wonderful opera!" Pacifico exclaimed, relieved to be able to engage her this way. "It overflows with emotion. I saw it in Naples."

"I haven't seen it," she said, drawing back a strand of hair that had fallen across her cheek. "That's why I decided to read the book."

"And how do you like the book?"

"It's an interesting story of society, but sentimental. My teacher advised against reading it because of the immorality."

"Oh. Well. I. Well. What are your favorite operas?"

"I've seen only *Cinderella*. That's by Rossini. —I'm afraid I interrupted your discussion of socialism with your companion," she added.

When Grasso came out he found Pacifico and Marianna standing under the chestnut tree, talking, while the little sister idly opened and collapsed the parasol, then opened it again, a frown of concentration on her face. Grasso walked over, took one of the two empty chairs and dragged it to another part of the shade under the tree. Fifteen minutes later Marianna began her walk home, the empty basket loose on her arm and the upright parasol in her other hand. Pacifico watched her and without turning to look for Grasso, he asked, "Who is she?"

"Marianna Moretti. I take it you didn't spend all your time discussing economics or North America."

"She's amazing."

"Her father's a fisherman but rather well off. If there are fish in the sea they swim into his nets first. If there are any straggler fish, they might get netted by the other boats, or might not. No one knows why he's so lucky with fish. They sent Marianna to school, which was the right thing to do, but after she was finished they got her a tutor, which, you know, may have been too much. Now she walks around with a French parasol. That's how she is. She's pretty, if you like her type, but restless."

"No, no, no, not restless, *ambitious*," said Pacifico. He asked Grasso for a bit of paper, so they went inside and the baker tore a strip from a blank page in his account book. Pacifico wrote in his neatest, most careful script — *You have stolen my heart, P. Cavallù*. Then he pulled a wad of dough from somebody's unbaked loaf, folded it around the paper and placed it on the pan beside Marianna's loaves. "When she comes back for the bread, make sure you put that in her hand, like that, with the end of the paper sticking out," he told Grasso.

77

Grasso looked at the lump of dough with the bit of paper sticking out like a tiny flag. "What's in the note?"

"Nothing."

"I'm not going to give that young woman something to read unless I know what it is. I'm not a fool and neither is her father." He unfolded the dough, read the line, refolded the dough around the paper. He sighed. "It's got your name on it. If her father gets ahold of it, only God knows what will happen."

"If she reads it before she gets home, he'll never see it. Make sure she reads it, that's all. —Now I have to go," Pacifico said, sweeping aside the curtain of beads in the doorway.

"She's going to be back later today to pick up her bread. Why don't you wait?"

"I have work to do and I want to be here tomorrow when she comes back."

"The Morettis aren't so rich they can bake bread every day. She won't be coming here tomorrow," Grasso said.

"She's smart. She'll be here tomorrow."

Marianna understood Pacifico's note and was back the next day. A year later Marianna and Pacifico were properly engaged and when Pacifico sailed from Palermo to the United States they began a correspondence that lasted until she, too, sailed from Palermo, and in 1904 Marianna Moretti and Pacifico Cavallù were married on the dock in Boston, Massachusetts.

9

ANGELO CAVALLÙ, born with the flanks and hind legs of a stallion, died of old age in 1900, died sitting in a plain wood chair under his favorite cork-oak in the courtyard of his home in Carco, Province of Palermo, Sicily. No one knew precisely how old he was and no one was able to recall when his family had arrived in Carco, only that they came from central Sicily. Despite the arthritis which afflicted him in old age, he and Ava made the difficult trip to Sicily's central region, the lands around Enna.

Enna is the place where Demeter, the warm breasted goddess of corn and grain, had her daughter Persephone stolen from her. Hades stalked slender Persephone, coming up behind her as quiet as a shadow, clamping a cold hand over her mouth and dragging her underground, after which her grief-crazed mother ceased to bless the harvest, so crops withered and nothing grew until Hades agreed to release Persephone, though only for half the year, for which six months Demeter allowed fields to bear again.

Angelo was interested in Demeter not for her grief — he'd seen enough of her grief in Maria, Sorrowful Mother of Jesus — but because she had mated with

Poseidon and given birth to Arion, the horse. Nowadays Poseidon is known as the god of the sea, but back then, when the world was new, Poseidon was the god of horses. Demeter had been fascinated by his rippling power and gentleness, had caressed the dark hair that trailed over the nape of his neck like a storm cloud, and in their passion they mounted each other this way and that way for a whole year — bringing forth the horse, Arion, and a daughter whose name cannot be said. Angelo had long ago guessed that the blood of Poseidon flowed in his veins and had gone to Enna with the hope of finding others like himself and, maybe, his true ancestry. He was unsuccessful.

Stella DiMare, widow of Franco Morelli but still a woman so beautiful her looks could stun, was carried away by the tidal wave that swept the port of Reggio Calabria in 1908. At 5:20 in the morning of December 28th, the Monday after Christmas weekend, a colossal earthquake began to rumble beneath the waters that separate Sicily from the toe of Italy, and beneath the cities of Messina and Reggio, collapsing walls, toppling towers and flattening houses until both cities were rubble. Ages ago people there said earthquakes were Poseidon's work, and called him Poseidon, Earth-Shaker. In 1908 maybe 100,000 or 200,000 people died, no one knows how many. The quake shook the center of Reggio to pieces, crushing to death about 35,000 out of 40,000 people. Immediately afterward a huge wave swept into the port of Reggio to demolish the harbor front and, as

it rolled out, Stella was seen carried upon its back
— seated as if she were riding side-saddle, somebody
said — and turning toward the devastated city she
raised her arms in a slow, broad embrace or gesture
of good-bye. She was among those never seen again.
Today the streets of Reggio make a neat grid and the
inner city has been wholly recomposed with fine ex-
amples of Art Nouveau, neo-classical, neo-Gothic,
Fascist, and contemporary architecture.

10

ALDO AND MOLLY MET BY ACCIDENT on
Monday, January 10, 1910, in Boston. At
the sound of her shouting he had come rushing up the stairway — past the gentleman stumbling
down with his hand cupped under his bloody nose
— pushed open the door and saw Molly who cried,
"Another one?" Aldo ducked when she threw, so her
scissors stabbed the door frame where they vibrated
with a thrumming sound. "I'm come to rescue. Not
to fear me," Aldo told her. "What makes you think
I'm afraid!" she said, tucking in her blouse. They
heard the thunder coming from the foot of the stairway. "Your friends are coming," Aldo said reassur-
ingly. Molly slammed shut the door and turned the
key in the lock, saying, "It's the bitch and her halfwit
son coming to crack our heads."

"I think we shall go," Aldo told her, looking
around. There was a dressmaker's dummy in the corner, a table heaped with ledgers and papers, and by
the wall a fancy brass bed over which hung a picture
of the Virgin Mary with her arms out, ready for an
embrace.

"And who are *you*?" Molly asked him

Aldo jammed a chair under the doorknob. "We
shall go out the window," he said. He shoved the

window up and cold air poured into the room. "It's not far," he added, looking down to the alley. He turned to Molly and said, "Give me your hands and I can —"

"I can do this myself!" she told him. She straddled the window sill, twisted herself to face outward and teetered there a moment. Aldo muttered something, snatched her wrists and, lowering her as far as he could, dropped her onto the shallow crust of snow. Then he dropped down beside her, or beside where she had been, for she was already gone. Aldo caught up with her as they came out to the street. They trotted along the crowded sidewalk, Molly always half a step ahead. "Young lady —" he began to say.

She stopped and whirled on him. "*What do you want?*"

"You have no coat. You will freeze," he told her.

"I'm not going back there, if that's what you mean!"

"I will get it for you," he said. Aldo had already started to take off his coat, to give it to her, but she waved it off.

"Grand. You and Saint Michael go back and fetch me my coat. —Don't say I didn't warn you," she called after him.

Aldo ran back down the street and returned a few minutes later with her coat which felt so like a thin rag in his hand that he was embarrassed at the weight of his Chesterfield with its lustrous black velvet collar. Molly said thank you, slipped into her coat and turned away.

"I hope you will come with me to lunch," he said.

She shrugged, turned back to him and said, "Sure. Why not?"

The first time they had a good look at each other was when they were seated at a table at Sweeney's. Molly's face was milk white, but her high cheeks were such a fiery blaze that he wanted to reach out and feel their heat. Aldo's face was dark and ugly — or maybe just dark, Molly couldn't decide. "You're an Eye-talian," she announced.

"Yes. In this country I'm an Italian."

"And what would you be in Italy?"

Aldo had a dazzling smile. "In Italy I would be a Sicilian."

"What's a sicilian?"

He laughed. "That's a long story."

When he laughed his face lighted up from inside — that's the way it looked to Molly.

"My name is Aldo Vela and I'm an aeroplano designer," he said. It was clear she didn't understand what he was talking about. "You know, aeroplano. Avion. A flying machine. I design it. Them. I design flying machines." His hands went soaring this way and that, over the table.

"You went to Mrs Faolain's to design flying machines. Oh, sure," she said.

"For cloth. Fabric for the wings. I'm looking here and there to find where they buy it. —And you are a seamstress. Miss—" Here he paused, waiting for her to give her name.

"Molly," she said at last.

"Ah!" He laughed, apparently delighted. "A beautiful name. Molly."

"And I'm an accountant, not a seamstress. Mrs Faolain keeps two sets of books. Or tries to, arithmetic being a great puzzle to her, but she thinks she's being cheated by somebody someplace, so she hired me to sort things out. That customer mistook me for one of her slut seamstresses. That's how he got his fat bloody nose. I'm telling you I'm tired of it."

"Oh," Aldo said, aware that he didn't have a good grasp of what she was telling him.

"I expect Faolain's got another set of books for the poor girls and the flashy gentlemen they take upstairs to the fitting rooms."

"Ah," he said slowly, as it became clear to him. "But you're an accountant," he added, brightening.

"Yes, and you're a designer of flying machines," she replied, tossing her hands around to parody his gestures.

During lunch Aldo asked how she had decided to become an accountant. "It's what I can do," she said. "I have a head for numbers and I know how to read a ledger. I knew my numbers before I knew the alphabet." She asked him what a sicilian was. He told her Sicily is an island and the unlucky people who live there are called Sicilians. "Italy is shaped like a big leg in a boot," he said. "And at the toe end of the boot is the island. The boot is kicking the island — that's Sicily — forever," he said, kicking his leg out. So he had got away, first to Torino, at the top of the Italian boot, where he had raced automobiles, then to France, where they made the best aeroplanes. Molly, too, had traveled, first from Mayo to Dublin, then to Canada. "A great Irish cemetery," she called Canada. "The city of Montreal is nothing but gray stones with priests and nuns tucked in between them. That's why I came down here. — Tell me about flying machines," she said, to change the subject. He laughed. "What would you like to know?" he asked her. They talked and talked and when they finally stood up Aldo swept Molly's chair aside and helped her into her coat, taking the opportunity to study her shimmering copper-colored hair such as he had never seen before, not even in Venice. Out on the sidewalk he said he'd like to see her again. She gave him the address of her rooming house. "You can come by on a Sunday afternoon and Mrs Murphy will give you permission to wait in the front hall at the foot of the stairs. They'll think you're Eye-talian, because they don't know about Sicily. Tell them you've come to go walking with Molly O'Neill and don't say anything else."

Aldo was twenty-five years old. The famous day he met Molly he was wearing his French three-piece suit and he had money in his pocket, but things weren't going well. The expensive coat wasn't his. He owned a cheap coat, one change of clothes, two pairs

87

of Zeiss racing goggles, one pair of leather driving gloves, a silver pocket-watch and a suitcase holding the detailed plans for an aeroplane. He ate with his relatives, the family of Pacifico and Marianna Cavallù, in their second-floor flat on Prince Street in the Italian section of Boston. At night he slept on a canvass cot in the back room of Pacifico's general store. During the day he helped at the store or studied his English language manual or borrowed Pacifico's lavish Chesterfield coat and visited Pacifico's business friends and their acquaintances, trying to get them to invest in his aeroplane enterprise. Frankly, he was getting discouraged and restless. The men he saw were eager to meet somebody who had flown through the air and lived to talk about it, and some were even curious about his proposal to build flying machines, but when they learned that Aldo didn't have an aeroplane — No? Not even one? Only those complicated mechanical drawings? — they lost interest and sank back in their chairs. Occasionally, for solace, he would visit a friend who owned a motor garage, and there among the consoling familiar smell of gasoline and the basso *bumbumbumbumbumbum* arias of pistons they would talk about engines.

As for Molly, she was about twenty-three and when she met Aldo she was in a tan shirtwaist with plain business cuffs and she had another, just like it, hanging in the corner of her room. All her other belongings were in her suitcase which the landlady, Mrs Murphy, kept locked in an unheated room by the kitchen. When Molly wanted a change of clothes, Mrs Murphy would unlock the room and watch as Molly took one garment from the suitcase and replaced it with another — that was Mrs Murphy's House Rule 1 — so if Molly or any other woman left without paying her rent, she left without her suitcase. Molly made enough from her job as book keeper at Faolain's Fine Fabrics to pay for her room and one meal a day and still have pocket money left over. Of course, after having given that fancy Dan a bloody nose, and after having kneed another gentleman in the groin two days earlier and having slapped one across the face a week ago, she didn't have that job anymore.

On Sunday afternoon Aldo and Molly rode the trolley and subway to the Boston Public Gardens which, of course, were frozen solid. They walked the shoveled paths and stood on the little bridge over the swan-boat pond, looked at the gray ice, the empty trees and the fading sky. "What's it like in Paris in winter?" she asked.

"It's gray. More gray even than Boston."

"What about Torino?" she asked a moment later.

"In winter? Not much better. But fine in the mountains, if you like mountains."

"I thought Italy was sunny and warm."

"In the summer, yes. Especially where I come

from."

"Sicily," she announced.

"Brava, Molly! Yes, Sicily," he said, using the English word. "In the summer, in August, it's so hot, if you pick up a drinking glass that has been too long in the sun it will scorch your hand. And the sirocco, when it blows from Africa, the wind carries sand from the desert and the sky turns yellow with sand."

She laughed. "Oh, sure! Sand blows over from Africa."

"It's true, it's true! The sand gets everywhere, like powder. You can comb it from your hair. You can feel it in your teeth when you bite." He snapped his jaws shut and made a show of grinding his teeth. "It's true."

"All the way from Africa to Sicily. And Ireland, you know, is made of emeralds."

"It's not that far!" he protested. "In Italy they say we are Africans."

Molly looked at him, taking in his dark face. "Lucky Aldo. You can pass for Eye-talian in this country."

Aldo, distracted by her gaze — she had clear green eyes — lost his tongue for a moment. "Tell me about Dublin," he said.

"Dublin is a sewer, but much improved from what it used to be," she said. "Or so I was told."

They walked through the frozen Gardens — there were only a few people, coat collars up, hurrying this way or that — and crossed the street to Boston

Common where a ragged man, poking at a fire in an iron barrel, was selling roasted chestnuts from a soot-blackened tray. Aldo bought a small bagful of chestnuts. "Here," he said, giving a hot chestnut to Molly. "Put this in your glove, inside. And this. To keep your hands warm." Fifty years later she could still tell you about those warm chestnuts.

"What happened to your good coat?" she asked. "The one with the velvet collar."

"It belongs to my cousin Pacifico."

She put her arm through his and they walked to the subway. "How was the flying machine business this past week?" she asked.

Aldo shrugged and wagged his hand. "So-so. I hate asking for investors. It's too much like begging."

"I hate looking for work."

"The Aviation Meet began the same day we meet, you and I. Did meet. A big aviation show. That was a famous day. Did I tell you?"

"What aviation show?"

"In Los Angeles. You know Los Angeles?"

"I know Dublin and Montreal and Boston."

"The meeting goes on for ten days. Everybody flies. Louis Paulhan is there winning prizes. I met him in France."

"Aldo, tell me this about your machine — if you haven't built it, how do you know it will fly?"

He laughed and squeezed her arm hard in his, relishing the solid feel of her flesh and bone through the cloth. "I know, because I designed it."

* * * * *

The Los Angeles Aviation Meet was a spectacular event displaying all sorts of fantastic aircraft. Glenn Curtiss, already famous for his speed, won prizes for the fastest flight with a passenger aboard and for the swiftest start. His flying student, Charlie Willard, won at precision take off and landing. Aldo's acquaintance, Louis Paulhan, set new altitude and endurance records and came away with the most prize money, over fourteen thousand dollars. Aldo respected Curtiss because he designed and flew his own aircraft, biplanes that were pushed by a powerful water-cooled 4- or 8-cylinder engine, but Aldo didn't care for the look of Curtiss's planes, boxy constructions of struts and wires with a clutter of air control surfaces, nor did he like the huge Farham that Paulhan sometimes flew, another powerful pusher with a roaring 7-cylinder radial engine. He loved the lighter Bleriot monoplane with its 3-cylinder engine up front and its elegant outstretched wings — true, you might get a whiff of exhaust, but that was better than having the engine slam into you from behind when you made a crash landing. He had designed his own plane along those lines. He had hoped that the news of the Los Angeles Air Meet would encourage businessmen and entrepreneurs to invest in aeroplanes, but they didn't, at least not in

Boston. Los Angeles was far, far away and the flying machines in the newspapers were as remote and
implausible as the sunny Los Angeles weather. In
February Aldo went to the Aero Show at Mechanics
Hall (demolished around 1960) and was able to examine a biplane made by a yacht builder from nearby
Marblehead. It was a sturdy craft and looked like it
might be air worthy, but it had never flown and was
oddly designed with half a dozen vertical fins along
the upper wing. The builder, Mr William Starling
Burgess was there, too, a rich Yankee with a ruddy
face, and Aldo didn't go near him.

Aldo and Molly were fast going broke. One Sunday afternoon, in a corner of the Museum of Fine
Arts where they had gone to get warm, Molly un-
pinned her intricately braided hair, combing from
it every bit of jewelry ever given to her (not much,
really: three gold rings, a pair of gold ear rings, a
copper fibula, two enameled brooches, and a silver
chain with silver Celtic cross) which she had hidden
in there so she could smuggle all past her landlady,
for Molly was behind in her rent and was preparing to decamp from Mrs Murphy's rooming house.
Molly wouldn't accept the money Aldo offered to
give her or loan her or whatever, so he went around
to Faolain's Fine Fabrics to get Molly's back wages

for her. Mrs Faolain gave a short harsh laugh and told him to get lost, told him if he or his whore ever came through that door again she'd have the police on them. Aldo vaulted the counter, yanked open the till, counted out Molly's back wages and vaulted the counter again, but by then Mrs Faolain's carbuncled son and two other louts were running at him. Aldo grabbed the smallest one by the wrist and whirled him around, twisting the kid's arm up his back. *"Get out of my way by God I break his arm off!"* Aldo barked, jerking the arm up so far the kid danced on tiptoe, trembling and pale. The other two wavered and Aldo hurled the kid head-first at them and shot out the door.

Molly kept hunting for a job as an accountant, but the small shops would never let anyone outside the family look at the books, if they kept any books, and the big companies weren't hiring — not women accountants, anyway. "What they want is a man in a green eyeshade with garters on his sleeves," Molly said. In late February she went to the garment district and began cutting cloth and breathing lint fifty-six hours a week in the same small sweatshop she had worked in when she first came to Boston. Aldo offered her money again, telling her that at the end of the workday at least she could return to a decent room. "No!" she said sharply. *"I don't want your money! Who do you think I am?"* They had stepped inside the Boston Public Library to get warm and her voice rang against the stone pillars and marble mosaic. Aldo flushed, as if he had been slapped. "Una donna tenuta!" he said. "You think I want to make you a kept woman! Is that what you think?"

"I didn't mean it that way. Come back here, Aldo!" she cried, catching his shoulder and kissing his neck as he turned away.

That spring Aldo not only worked in Pacifico's store, but he got another job as well. He got this other job when he was at his friend Tito's motor garage looking at a new Firestone-Columbus automobile — an unusual automobile with a fifty-inch track, six inches narrower than most, and the steering wheel on the left, unlike other vehicles. Aldo had taken off his jacket, folded back his cuffs, and was examining the engine, a four-cylinder high-speed job, when in walked the owner, a tall angular Yankee named Blanchard. Blanchard thought Aldo was one of the mechanics and after talking with him about the car Blanchard asked if Aldo could turn it into a racing vehicle. Tito came over and said, "Yes, we can make it into a racing car, no problem." Tito and Aldo worked on it nights, removed the fenders and head lamps, braced the frame and put in a bucket seat. Tito asked Blanchard where he was going to race. "Not me," Blanchard said. "Maybe I own a race horse, but that doesn't mean I'm a jockey. Someone else will have to drive this buggy."

"I can drive it for you," said Aldo. "I used to race cars in Torino."

The race was on Cape Ann, a private road race from Gloucester up the shore road to Rockport and down the inland road back to Gloucester. Aldo drove recklessly well and finished less than a second behind the winner, out of the money. But Blanchard was pleased, gave him a two-hundred-and-fifty-dollar bonus above his pay for the race and asked would he drive for him on Long Island. Aldo was now richer than he'd ever been since leaving France. He said Thank you and No. He knew the best drivers in the world would be competing in Mr Vanderbilt's race and Blanchard would pay him well simply to be there, but he hadn't been interested in speed since he began to fly. The exhilaration of automobile racing was in the speed — it was all about going fast in the dirt, while flying was about sky and air and he was starved for that. "And now I have a thing to show you," Aldo said. The next day Aldo showed him the detail drawings for his aircraft. "I'm impressed," Blanchard told him. "But I'm committed elsewhere. —By the way, who drew these plans?"

"I did, of course," said Aldo.

Blanchard spoke to one of his friends and a week later Aldo was offered a job in the drafting department of a bridge fabricating company. Drafting is tedious pains-taking work — make one blot or smear and you've ruined the whole damned sheet — and it's not at all like flying, but he took the job.

* * * * *

So Molly and Aldo came to know each other, told each other where they had come from, what they had done — some of what they had done, anyway. Aldo's mother was a beautiful woman and *her* mother, a goddess so beautiful her looks could stun a man. That woman, his grandmother, never aged and was an embarrassment to her daughters until the tidal wave of 1908 rose up in the port of Reggio and carried her away, somebody said, as if she were riding a horse. Aldo's father was a teacher, journalist and poet who, among other achievements, wrote a poem about Daedalus and Icarus, but in Sicilian, which limited its readership and, unfortunately, he never quite finished it. He was beaten one night by Premier Francesco Crispi's thugs who threw him into a filthy prison cell where he died the next morning. Crispi, you should know, intended to restore energy and virility to Italy by stamping out socialists and everyone else who disagreed with him. One day when Aldo was a boy his mother pointed out the villa of the man who had ordered the beating. After that she sold everything they owned and moved from Sicily as far as she could, settling in the distant city of Torino where Aldo later attended the Scuola di Applicazione per gli Ingegneri (Technical School for Engineers), became infatuated with automobile engines, did some racing and won a few, then crossed over to France because that's where they were making flying machines and he had fallen in love with flying. Shortly after that his mother married Giancarlo Mattei, a rather young industrialist.

"She'll not be lonely in her old age and that's good," Molly said.

"I can assure you my mother has not been lonely for the last ten years," Aldo told her.

"Ah, you don't care for Mr Mattei?"

"I behaved badly when I first met him and it became a habit. He's all right. He paid for a Bleriot flying machine he knew I wanted, but I refused it. Maybe I was wrong. It's stored in crates at a factory in France."

As for Molly, her father was a part-time typesetter and part-time horse trader with one patched boot in the city and the other in horse shit. Her mother, a country school teacher with a love of poetry and a fine singing voice, was herself an O'Neill from county Tyrone. "We have in our veins the blood of Irish kings, we O'Neills, including the one who captured Saint Patrick, and if that O'Neill had more than a boulder between his ears he would have killed the old man and saved Ireland a lot of grief." Before Molly was born her mother had given birth to five boys — two died as infants, one talked sedition at a meeting of the Irish Republican Brotherhood and was killed in a brawl outside a pub the same night, another became a merchant seaman and poet, and the last inherited the farm. When Molly was fifteen her mother died of TB and a couple of years later Molly went to Dublin to escape her father's rage and to live with her cousin Peggy who, two years later, gave her own papers to Molly so she could sail to Canada.

11

IN MAY OF 1910 ALDO AND MOLLY were married in a civil ceremony. The marriage certificate — an 8 by 11.5 inch sheet of paper, folded, and now falling apart at the creases — with elaborate print and elegant handwriting, says Aldo Vela and Moira O'Neill were *united in* MARRIAGE *according to the Laws of the State of Massachusetts*, and the back of the document bears the bright red seal of the Justice of the Peace. They couldn't live in the Italian North End, partly because all of Aldo's friends and relatives spoke Italian and Molly didn't understand more than five words, and partly because the rooms and hallways were filled with strange cooking smells that made her gag. Aldo took her to an Italian restaurant where she tasted little bites and, as she didn't get sick, the next Sunday they ate at the Cavallù's crowded table where everyone talked at once, Pacifico kept slapping her shoulder and roaring with laughter, Molly drank too much wine and Marianna held her while she threw up in the kitchen sink and the children came running to watch.

The newlyweds rented a third-floor, cold-water flat (bedroom, kitchen, sitting room — tenants' toilet bowl, out and down the hall) over by the Fort Point Channel in a hodgepodge neighborhood of Yankees,

Irish, Italians, Syrians, Greeks and, at the end of the street, Chinese. Boys played stick-ball in the street, girls played hopscotch on the sidewalk, and the old folks sat on the stoop, keeping an eye on everyone. In the evening, Aldo would take off his jacket, necktie and collar, tuck a dish towel in his belt for an apron, and cook dinner — that way he could let Molly rest, wean her from those Irish scraps she ate and feed her decent Sicilian food. Two weeks later Molly found a job as a clerk-secretary in the accounting office of a brick company, which paid more and was less tiring than the sweatshop, but Aldo continued to cook anyway.

A formal photograph (taken at the *Broadway Studio, 913 Washington St. Boston*) from around this time shows Molly and Aldo in almost identical suit jackets, white shirts and upright starched collars, the only difference being that Molly wears a ribbon bow tie, stiff and flat, whereas Aldo has a four-in-hand. And here they are in June — not in a photo but in reality — on a hot Sunday afternoon, lolling on their open bed sheet, Aldo with a towel across his privates and Molly in a chemise. "I'm happy," Aldo announced. "Very happy. —I can almost believe in God," he added.

"Does Saint Thomas list this as one of the proofs of God?" Molly asked, her voice languid.

"I don't think so." He laughed. "Saint Thomas's book is so long, I think he spent all day and all night writing it and had no time for this. Besides, he was celibate."

"Fancy that," Molly murmured. "Celibate."

"Maybe there is a God." He thought about it a while, sighed. "You never know. Maybe there are many."

"If there is a God he's lazy or cruel, I don't know which. God had a long time to fix things, but in the end it was the garment workers union did it. Did something, anyway."

"You are cynical, Molly." Aldo got up, wrapping the towel around his waist at the same time. "It's very strange I'm so restless. I'm more happy for the first time in my life and I'm ready to do. I'm very ready. Maybe that's happiness." At the bureau he opened a small cardboard box and took a cigar.

"The Italians are the only ones who smoke those little things," Molly said.

"And Sicilians," Aldo added, opening the match box. He lit the cigar and came back to sit on the edge of the bed.

"They look like twisted twigs dipped in tar," she said, kneeling up behind him.

Aldo smiled and breathed out a soft plume of smoke. "They're not elegant. Neither am I."

"Oh, yes you are, Aldo, yes you are," she said, pressing against his back, wrapping her arms around his neck. "My elegant Sicilian boyo."

Later Molly was at the dresser combing her hair while Aldo went on talking about Glen Curtiss who, last Sunday, had flown from Albany, in upstate New York, southward to New York City and Governors Island. "He followed the river down to the city. That's a hundred and fifty miles, you know." Aldo said.

"Yes," said Molly, "I know. You told me. Two or three times."

"Which is about two hundred and fifty kilometers," he continued.

"And he won ten thousand dollars," she recited.

"And the glory."

"The money would be nice even without the glory," she said.

"Paulhan won ten thousand pounds, the British money, in that London to Manchester flight," he told her.

"And we like Paulhan better than Curtiss, right?"

"Right. —By the way, I think Pacifico wants to invest in my flying machine."

"Is that what you two were talking about?"

"He asked how much I was making at my job and asked if I could afford to build my flying machine. He said he wanted to discuss something financial with me next Sunday."

＊ ＊ ＊ ＊ ＊

Pacifico Cavallù was five years older than Aldo. Aldo sometimes called him his cousin but, strictly speaking, they weren't cousins. Pacifico's wife, Marianna, was the daughter of Diva, who was the sister of Morgana, who was the mother of Aldo. So Aldo and Marianna were cousins.

Pacifico had arrived alone in Boston's North End eight years earlier with the names and addresses of a couple of other men who had come over from Carco, plus a letter of credit from a bank in Palermo for a sum of money which he calculated would pay his expenses for six months. He rehearsed the English his mother had taught him, looked for work and was signed up by a New Englander named Bowman who was rounding up laborers for a train ride to Maine where they would hack a road into the woods, the cost of the train ticket being deducted from their first week's wages. Three months later Pacifico was back in Boston with calluses on his hands, this time speaking more English and working along side Bowman to gather another dozen Italians for road building. Pacifico and Bowman came back to Boston a month after that with enough money to buy train tickets for two dozen workers, Pacifico acting again as his go-between and this time convincing Italians fresh off the boat to line up for a ride to their new jobs in the Maine woods. A month later the pair were back in the North End of Boston once more, but after they had corralled two dozen Italians and after Pacifico had got his pay, he and Bowman shook hands and said goodbye, Bowman herding the new workers to the railroad station while Pacifico walked down Prince Street to a general store he had looked into on his previous trips. The store was owned and managed by an Italian who didn't speak English as well as Pacifico, so Pacifico took over the task of dealing with the American suppliers, talking to them, writing business letters and getting acquainted with how stores worked in New England. Nine months after getting the job he made his first payment toward buying the store and wrote a letter that night to Marianna, telling her he was now well established in Boston and they could marry as soon as she came over. Marianna booked passage as soon as she could and came down the gangway onto the dock in wintry Boston early in 1904, accompanied by her mother, Diva, who returned to Sicily only after having seen for certain that Pacifico did not have another wife in this country and that her daughter was properly married. By 1910 Marianna had borne four children and Pacifico owned not only the general store but the building it was housed in and he was beginning to think about money the way a composer might think about music, not dismissive of the mathematics of it but focused avidly on composing a great structure by the power of his imagination.

Now Pacifico and Aldo sat at the corner of Pacifico's dining table, which had been cleared of everything except their after-dinner espresso cups plus a platter bearing a rope of figs and a handful of walnuts. "I'm starting a travel business and an import business," Pacifico said quietly in Italian. "Want to join me?"

"Join you? Me?" Aldo was stunned.

"I'd provide the capital, of course."

"Pacifico, I'm an aeroplane designer, a flyer."

Pacifico looked at him skeptically. "You've found

investors?"

"No."

"Then the flying machine can come later. You have a wife and soon you'll have children." He was decisive.

"That's why I have to do this now, not later," Aldo told him, slapping the table top for emphasis.

Pacifico was amazed. "Then your answer is *no*?"

Aldo hesitated, searching for a way to say no without hurting Pacifico's feelings. "I've already ordered an engine from France," Aldo said.

"Ah," said Pacifico. He gazed meditatively at the cigar in his hand, then gently tapped the ash into the saucer of his espresso cup. He doubted that Aldo had even thought of ordering an engine.

"A Gnome rotary. It's the best kind," Aldo added.

It grew quiet in the dining room. Kids' voices floated up from the street below the open window; Molly and Marianna were speaking English in the kitchen.

"I'm sure you'll do well," Pacifico said at last. He relaxed, adjusted himself comfortably in his chair. "And your wife is Irish — that could be an advantage. I had no idea when I came here that the city was run by the Irish."

Aldo smiled. "Molly has no connections here. She's an Irish woman who married a Sicilian and not even in church. She has friends, of course, but no connections."

"Ha! The Irish. The men are *mascanzuni* and their

women are holy virgin mothers. —You have financing plans for your flying machine?"

"I'll improvise."

Pacifico laughed and slapped Aldo on the shoulder. "Bravo! Like Garibaldi."

"Exactly."

That evening Aldo told Molly, "Now I know what I'm ready to do and why I'm so restless and even more happy." Early the next morning he sent a cablegram to the Société Des Moteurs Gnôme in France ordering a 7-cylinder rotary Gnome Omega engine, after which he detoured to Tito's motor garage to tell him about the engine — "Can I set it up in here?" Aldo asked. "Sure, if I get to play with it too," Tito said. Thence to his job at the New England Iron Bridge Company where, in the long room in which he worked there was a disused drafting table heaped with busted drafting equipment, so Aldo bought the table and everything on it for two dollars, and at the end of the workday had it carted to his apartment where he crowded it into their little sitting room. After dinner he drew the first full-size template for a wing rib while Molly looked over his shoulder.

✳ ✳ ✳ ✳ ✳

The engine arrived in July. The mechanic, Tito (for the record: his full name was Benedetto Evangelista Campi), was a short but well proportioned

106

man, rather like a jockey. He'd never touched a rotary engine, had never even seen one, but from Aldo's description of how it worked he guessed the inventor must have been a comedian. Every engine he had worked on had a row of cylinders in which pistons shot up and down, and the pistons were linked to a drive shaft, so their motion rotated the shaft which turned a power wheel. But in the rotary engine the cylinders were arrayed in a vertical circle, like numerals on a clock face, and each piston was connected to the drive shaft that passed through the center of the circle. But the drive shaft didn't rotate. When the engine started and the pistons began to fire up and down, the shaft stayed absolutely still while the engine itself — the cylinders and pistons, the linkages to the drive shaft, the stream of lubricating oil — the whole insane engine rotated around what should have been the drive shaft. Tito and Aldo worked on the engine five nights in a row and then five more — tore it down and reassembled it — and late in the afternoon on Saturday they had it ready to test. It started with a *bang-bang-bang*, then fell silent, jerking and bobbing on the test stand. That happened four times. On the fifth try it started with the usual *bang-bang-bang* and then burst into a wonderfully rapid thundering drum roll — such music! Aldo tossed his oil rag in the air and shouted *Bravissimo!* while Tito stared at the blurred whirl and began to laugh.

Months ago Aldo had found a cabinet maker who said he and his son would be willing to work eve-

nings, and Tito knew of an empty motor garage —
actually a disused horse stable the owner had hoped
to rent out as a garage — in which they could assemble the wood and wire frame of the aircraft. Aldo
had decided on American spruce, a strong and rea-
sonably light wood. He'd never chosen which fabric
to cover the frame with because, you recall, when
he'd last been looking at cloth he'd heard a woman
shout from upstairs, had dashed to the rescue and
vaulted out the window behind her, his Molly. Since
then he'd gotten in touch with a cousin, a tailor from
Palermo whose father, also a tailor, had opened a
shop in Cambridge many years ago. It turned out
the father had died and the son, Enzo Capellino,
was supporting his widowed mother and his two sisters — both sisters were getting married next year
and both needed dowries — so, yes, the tailor would
work nights, stretching fabric over the frame.

Now Aldo would roll out of bed early, shave, drink
a cup of cold coffee and hurry to the stable to work for
two hours, then hop a trolley to his job at the bridge
company, and in the evening, after a brief dinner,
he'd return to the stable where he'd meet the cabinet
maker and his son, and usually Tito would show up,
simply to help. As for Molly, after a day at the brick
works she'd come home and prepare dinner — Irish
corned beef or cold potato soup, Italian everything
else. One evening she went to a free lecture at the
union hall with Kate from the garment factory, and
a couple of times she went to a slide-show at the library with her friend Maureen from Mrs Murphy's

rooming house, but usually she sat outside on the front steps and read. The flats were hot as ovens, so everybody came out to get air, bringing a kitchen chair or just sitting on the front stoop until long after the gaslights came on in the dark.

At bedtime, while Aldo was hunched over his drafting table again, Molly would wash up, slip into her chemise, tie her hair in paper curlers. But tonight instead of going to bed she opened the cardboard Parodi box on the bureau and took out a cigar. It tasted oddly sweet on her tongue. She struck a match, lighted the cigar, inhaled, choked, coughed, then padded barefoot behind Aldo and blew a stream of smoke over his shoulder. "Mr Engineer, what do you do if your flying machine crashes?" she asked him.

"Hey! Oh, Molly, Molly, Molly. *You're smoking a cigar.*"

"I can see there's no fooling you." Her eyes had begun to water from the smoke and she held the cigar up away from her face. "Please take this vile thing."

"Hey, you're going to set your hair on fire," he said, taking the cigar.

"What if it crashes?"

"What do you mean? My machine? The one I'm making?" He was astonished. "It won't crash."

"But what if it crashes and you get hurt?"

"I've crashed before. Everyone who flies has a few crashes. Nobody gets hurt. —You're beautiful, even with those papers in your hair."

"Don't distract me, Aldo. You never told me you crashed."

He laughed. "It's nothing to brag about. I was just learning to fly. I'm like *you*, I'm not afraid."

"But it's only some thin, thin cloth holding you up in the air."

"That night dress is only some thin, thin cloth, but it works. Also, you're beautiful. Is it true the lace is made by Irish nuns?" Aldo had begun unbuttoning his shirt.

Molly glanced down at her lacy bodice. "I hope not."

"Here. Hold the cigar. I'm going to wash. —Santos-Dumont built a fine aeroplane out of bamboo poles and thin cloth. He was the first to fly." He stepped into the kitchen and turned on the tap water.

"It was the Wright brothers were the first to fly, you know."

"That's what they say now," he said from the kitchen. "But Santos-Dumont is a better man, more simpatico. And a generous heart."

Molly sat on the edge of the bed and blew a plume of smoke toward the ceiling. "You can't say he was the first to fly just because he's a nicer man."

When Aldo had finished scrubbing himself at the sink he came to the bedroom, naked save for the towel around his waist. "The Wright brothers have no passion. —Come here, signorina." Aldo took the cigar from Molly and stubbed it out in the ashtray on the bureau. "Do you know what's on my mind?"

he asked her.

"Yes." She laughed and looked into his eyes. "Should I be afraid?"

* * * * *

The next evening Molly accompanied Aldo to the old horse stable to see the flying machine which at that point looked like nothing much. Aldo told her the part resting on saw horses was the body; it looked like a delicately constructed ladder lying on its side, maybe ten times longer than it was wide. "On an aeroplane like this one, the French call it the *fuselage*," he explained. The two identical wing sections, which would be joined to the fuselage to form the solitary wing, lay on long makeshift tables. "Beautiful, isn't it?" he said. "See how the wing swells up from the leading edge, that lovely curve up and then this gentle sweet descending slant to the trailing edge — that's where the beauty is."

Molly smiled at Aldo's pleasure in his own handiwork. "How did you know how much to curve it?"

"I looked around. I looked at Santos-Dumont's wing sections. I looked at birds, large birds that glide. Then I try for a beautiful line."

"I've been reading a library book about these flying machines and —," Molly began to say.

"Books, books! Books are full of theory —," Aldo said.

111

"This one is full of numbers and —"

"Numbers are even worse than theories!"

"But the Wright brothers —"

Aldo laughed. "Are there anybodies duller than the Wright brothers? I think not. Everybody in this country is wild about the Wright brothers and their ugly flying machine. In France we called those machines *canards*. In English that means goose. The Wright brothers have a machine that sticks way out in front the way a goose's head sticks out. And no wheels. Maybe it's more like a flying sled."

Molly smiled. "Aldo's aeroplane will be beautiful."

"Exactly!" He laughed.

"But before they flew, the Wright brothers performed many experiments and —"

"Ah, yes. Experiments. I'd rather fly. Those are my experiments. — Now let me introduce Enzo to you. He's the tailor I told you about. We're going to start cutting and fitting the fabric tonight. Enzo," he called. "Vieni qui."

Enzo, an energetic compact man with a downswept mustache, greeted Molly with a smile, saying, "Mi piace molto—.'

"In inglese," Aldo told him.

"How do you do, Signora Missus Vela!" Enzo said, bowing ever so slightly as he shook her hand.

* * * * *

Aldo's flying machine was ready to fly in late July or very early in August. No one remembers precisely when it was, only that it was a sunny breezeless Saturday and that Molly was wearing a green dress and had let her hair down because Aldo had once said he liked to see her bright hair against the green of that dress. The flying field was a freshly cut meadow in Lexington, a somnolent village about fifteen miles North West of Boston. (Paul Revere had ridden through in the early hours of April 19th, 1775, to awaken everybody, banging on doors and crying out that the British were coming, but the town had long since fallen back asleep.) It took Aldo, Tito and Enzo about forty minutes to uncrate and assemble the machine, then a half hour for Aldo to check and re-check every bolt and wire. Finally, Aldo climbed into the cockpit and they started the Gnome — a tricky, dangerous business.

Aldo taxied down the field, jouncing on the brown stubble while Tito jogged along side. At the far end of the meadow Tito turned the aircraft around and Aldo taxied swiftly up the field, coasting to a stop beside Molly and Enzo who together turned the machine around again. Aldo roared swiftly down the field, lifted gently into the air for a few seconds — rolling crazily this way and that — then settled down onto the field again. After a few level runs, never rising higher than twenty feet, Aldo said he was ready. Tito ran back up the field to join Molly and Enzo. Aldo smiled, gave them a casual salute and raised his voice over the steady drumbeat of the engine and shouted *I'm going now!* Molly smiled and waved broadly, waved hugely, and as soon as Aldo had turned away and the aeroplane began to move she thrust a hand inside her bodice and clutched the silver Celtic cross that hung there.

The aeroplane roared rapidly down the field and lifted gently into the air, skimmed over the scrubby bushes at the far end, rose higher and higher and began a very gentle turn to the right, disappearing beyond the nearby elm tree tops. The sound of the engine dropped to a muted patter and eventually the aeroplane reappeared against the distant sky beyond the barn at this end of the field, vanished behind more trees and after what felt like a long time it emerged above the far end of the meadow, having completed a wide languorous circle. Now the aeroplane turned toward the field, dipping a wing on the inside of the turn, but even as the aeroplane approached it began sliding gracefully sideways and down, as if following a path pointed at by the lowered wing tip. Molly and Tito were already running down the meadow when the flying machine landed to the sound of snapping wood and the crunch of the undercarriage. Aldo clambered out beside the smashed wing, pulling off his goggles and saying, "I'm all right, I'm all right."

"Your face has got —" Molly cried, out of breath, reaching for him.

"It's oil," he said, wiping his cheeks with his sleeve. "Oil from the engine. Tito, we need to add a wind-screen or something."

"*Gesù!*" Tito said, panting. "Che malu furtuna." What bad luck, he said, while Enzo, who was at the wrecked wing, called out that it wasn't so bad, not so bad. "Non c'é male."

"Oh! There's *blood*," Molly cried, "You're bleeding! Look."

"What? Where?" Aldo said. Then he laughed. "No, no, no. That's from your hand. Molly, Molly. You cut it. See?"

And, in fact, she had clutched the little Celtic cross so hard that it had sliced into her palm. "Love has made a coward of me," was all she said.

On a Sunday in August, warm and windless, Aldo took Molly up in his aeroplane. They had a private joke, those two, about the song "Come, Josephine, in My Flying Machine," which Molly had told him was the dirtiest song she had ever heard, though everyone was singing it. "Explain," Aldo had said, sitting up naked on the edge of the bed to light a cigar. So Molly knelt up — also naked, but holding the sheet to her breasts — and sang a few phrases which, in fact, could be taken two ways. Aldo blew a gust of smoke toward the ceiling and laughed. "Oh-ho! I'll remember that when I take you *up, up, a little bit higher*," he sang, handing her the cigar. But this Sunday, as she was seated and buckled in the aeroplane, he was not joking, not worried, but business-like. Then they rolled and bounced along the field with the roar of the engine, went faster and faster and sailed over the bushes and trees into airy space. After a while she saw she had entered a wondrous three-dimensionality, an expanding volume of light and air, and where she had lived before was gone beneath her, looking smaller and ever so flat.

* * * * *

Aldo's aeroplane was about twenty-three feet (seven meters) from nose to tail with a wingspan of twenty-eight feet (8.5 meters). His detailed drawings vanished long ago and these dimensions come from Molly's household account book, an ordinary school notebook with lined pages where she recorded each penny spent on codfish or trolley rides or anything else. She stopped tracking household expenses on Sunday, July 31, 1910 — they were flat broke, any-way —simply drew a double line under the monthly total and right below that, on August 8, she began to jot notes and numbers about the aeroplane. Molly believed in her heart that if she could pick out the right numbers and arrange them the right way a pat-tern would make itself visible, at least visible to her, and she would uncover the aeroplane's strength's and weaknesses, the same as in her accounting work. In Montreal she had become adept at gathering her employer's numbers by the bucketful (invoices, bank statements, accounts receivable) until they poured down the page, page after page, and where other people saw only the confused surface of a muddy river, she saw what those numbers meant, saw the dangerous snags and shallows underneath, and the safe way forward, though no one asked for what she knew.

Now she jotted down every number she could get about the aeroplane. Some parts were easy to assess — the weight of the Gnome rotary engine, 165 pounds (75 Kg) — but other parts were difficult to give a number to, such as that beautiful curved surface of the wing. She had measured the curve from front to back with her sewing tape, but it was the lovely curvature itself she wanted to calculate, not its simple dumb length.

"That's what keeps the aeroplane up in the air, isn't it?" she asked Aldo. "Because the air pushes up against the hollowed-out underside of the wing and keeps you, keeps the airplane, from falling — wouldn't you say?"

Molly in her nightdress, the one with the lace not made by Irish nuns, was at the kitchen table, writing in her notebook, and Aldo was seated behind her, bathing in an old metal washtub on the floor.

"I might say that, or I might not," he told her, soaping his chest, his belly, his privates.

"Or I might stab you, Aldo, with my pen!" She started to turn toward him, but faltered.

"When the aeroplane is on the field, the wheels

keep the nose up, so the wing is tilted up in front and down in back, like a kite. So when I start rushing down the field the aeroplane sails into the air like a kite." He stood up, took the kettle from the stove and poured the last of the hot water into the tub, sat down cautiously. "But when I'm flying along straight, the wind passing over the wing is as important as the wind under it."

She turned, prepared to look boldly at him. "Why?"

"Everyone has his own theory. That's why there are so many different flying machines. And many of them actually fly —" and here his hand, palm down, rolled from side to side — "more or less."

Her eyes had averted themselves all on their own, so she returned to her notebook. "What's Aldo's theory?"

"Aldo can't do theory and fly at the same time. Theories are for theoreticians and bicycle mechanics. The wing, *my* wing, mine is a great bird's wing!"

"You'll be wanting your gravestone to say it was birds inspired you?"

"And Louis Bleriot, also a great inspiration." Aldo heaved himself to his feet, letting the water sluice down, slosh and splash. "Towel, per piacere, please," he said.

Without turning, Molly handed him the towel — somewhat damp from her earlier use, it's true — and closed her notebook. "Another Frenchman you admire because he crashed so many times and lived to crash again."

AND HERE'S ALDO! "Do you know what we call this part when we are children, just little boys, in Italy?"

"*Oh!*" Molly clapped her hands over her eyes. "Now how would I know that?"

"It's called *ucellino*, meaning little bird." He began to laugh. "Oh? Are you blushing, Molly? Molly, Molly — my Molly!"

"Holy Mother of God, who have I married?" she said, keeping her eyes shut but throwing her arms around him, pressing her cheek to his hot wet chest.

12

ALDO HAD DECIDED TO ENTER THE Harvard-Boston Aero Meet which was going on from September the 3ʳᵈ to the 13ᵗʰ. He told Mr Argyle at the Iron Bridge Company, and Mr Argyle said that after the Aero Meet was over Aldo could apply to the drafting department and, if they were short handed, he could have his old job back, then he stood up behind his desk and briskly shook Aldo's hand. Aldo owed money all over Boston. He didn't know exactly how much he owed because at the end of every week he handed over his invoices and most of his cash to Molly, letting her pay this one or that one, or not pay, whatever she decided. They were now eating at Pacifico's table twice a week, taking home the leftovers wrapped in wax paper and skipping lunch most days. Frankly, Aldo didn't care what he had in his belly or his pocket so long as he was building his aeroplane, and as for Molly, she said, "I'm fine, I'm fine. I'm not eating tripe every night or hunting for coal by the railroad tracks, so what have I got to complain about?"

Aldo wasn't interested in competing for a prize at the Aero Meet; he wanted to demonstrate his aeroplane, sell it and find buyers for other aeroplanes he hoped to build. Best of all, at the Aero Meet he would re-join the brotherhood of flyers and possibly — who could tell? — talk again with people like his friend Louis Paulham. Of course, you know, Louis had exited the United States back in March, one running jump ahead of attorneys hired by the Wright brothers, but maybe someone from the Voisin factory would turn up, or Louis Bleriot himself. Every flyer in the world was invited but no one knew for certain who would actually be there, not even the organizers.

After all, anybody with money and a theory of flight could build a flying machine. Some constructed machines that flew like box kites or gliders, others assembled wings, maybe two or three, and stacked one above the other, but the trick was to control the flight so it didn't end in a crash. Some liked to control pitch by putting elevators in the tail, others had them on outriggers, left and right. Some popular designs had elevators cantilevered way out front of the main wing, so the aircraft looked like a flying duck, the *canard* design — and by the way, *canard* means duck, not goose, our Aldo was wrong about that. As for controlling turns, many designers followed the Wright brothers and used thin cables to warp the wings, twisting each wing somewhat up or down to increase or decrease the slice it took to the air, causing the aeroplane to turn left or right — let's be honest, causing the contraption to roll, slew and slide left or right.

Louis Bleriot, the same Bleriot who Aldo admired, designed his first flying machine around

1901. It had wings that flapped explosively but it never got off the ground. His second, a biplane on floats pulled by a motor boat, caught a wing in the water and smashed. His third had wings shaped like big bottomless tubs mounted in tandem like beads on a string — it never took off. But in his fourth, a *canard* design with varnished paper wings, he did fly six yards. After he crashed that one, Bleriot constructed an aircraft with two sets of wings, one behind the other, in which he flew many yards, climbed to sixty feet, stalled, crashed. He limped back to his drawing board and designed more machines. In 1907 he built his seventh aeroplane — called the Bleriot VII, of course — with the engine up front, wheels under the engine, a single pair of wings and a tail with a rudder and elevators. It flew. Indeed, all his subsequent planes flew, even the one with rice paper wings, though it's a fact he went crash, crash, crash, and crash. Early in the morning on July 25, 1909, Louis Bleriot climbed into his Bleriot XI in Calais, France, flew across the English Channel and landed in Dover, England — crash landed. He had become the first person to fly the English Channel, thereby winning £1,000 from the London *Daily Mail* and rescuing himself from bankruptcy.

Aldo Vela's 1910 aeroplane had its 50 horsepower Gnome rotary engine up front, the wings about shoulder height to the pilot, then the long fuselage with a rudder and elevators at the end. The only part of the fuselage that was covered with fabric was the section around the cockpits; the rest was bare to reduce drag, so it's true the aeroplane body looked like four delicate ladders laced together, edge to edge, by a fragile crisscross of piano wire. But the great wingspan, longer even than the fuselage, with its slightly uplifted wingtips, gave it a soaring birdlike appearance — a great, grand bird.

In August Aldo crashed three more times, during which he broke the left wing tip, collapsed the wheels, crushed the right wing tip, and busted the tail skid so often he finally replaced it with a wheel. The rotary engine was lubricated by oil shot from the crankcase to the cylinders and then sprayed out to the air where it was blown back into the pilot, so he designed a loose fitting semi-circular shield, or cowl, that fit over the top of whirling engine and deflected the oil — smelly castor oil, because castor oil didn't contaminate gasoline. Aldo made a hard landing at sunset on the first day of September, so the aeroplane was not ready by opening day of the Harvard-Boston Aero Meet.

But on Tuesday, the fourth day of the Aero Meet, Aldo and Tito did get there and assembled the aeroplane at Aviation Field. Along one margin of the field a crooked row of large boxy canvas tents housed the flying machines. Aldo had no tent, but he'd hung tarpaulin, roof-like, from four poles to shelter the engine and the cockpit of his aeroplane. Harvard Aviation Field was a temporary airdrome, a square mile of ragged turf on a flat patch of empty land that stretched into the southern waters of Boston Harbor. When they had finished assembling the aeroplane, Tito squinted across the field to study the grand-stand, then he took in the thin line of trees by the road and the flat expanse of grayish sea at the far end of the field. "Very uninteresting land," he said. "Nothing grows here, you know?"

"Who cares so long as it's flat?" Aldo said, wiping his hands on an oil rag. "I'm happy."

"And all these people who come to watch the meet. How is it they don't have to go to their jobs?"

"Stay here and admire the women's hats. I'll be back," Aldo said.

Aldo walked from tent to tent, partly to examine the other flying machines by mostly on the lookout for pilots, designers or mechanics from France or Italy. Forty minutes later he was back beside his Vela aeroplane.

"Well?" Tito said.

"Everybody is English. I found some French aero-planes, but nobody to talk with."

Molly came with her friend Kate, both of them calling out and waving from a distance as soon as they spied Aldo's place in the line of tents, and Enzo the tailor came in a handsomely cut suit and bowler hat, along with his two placid sisters in long coats. Pacifico and Marianna arrived somewhat later, and Pacifico had a hand-held Kodak camera that unfolded with a little bellows, so it could take fine photographs. Aldo made two demonstration flights that afternoon — soft landing each time — and for the remainder of the day he talked with Molly, his friends and relatives and whoever came by to ask questions about the aeroplane.

Molly returned to work at the brick company the next day, but was so distracted by clairvoyant thoughts of Aldo falling from the sky that she asked to be excused so she could go to the aero meet. She wasn't given leave, so she took off her paper cuffs, quit her job and made her way to the flying field. She knew her mere presence couldn't protect him, but she felt he was safer with her there, so every time Aldo took off she stationed herself at the edge of the field and traced his long slow flights, the steep leaning turns and flowing passages, herself as watchful as a sentry until he landed.

One morning when Aldo was tightening wires along the fuselage he heard two young men questioning Tito, or trying to. One of the men wore a stiff straw boater and the other was hatless. What they heard from Tito was — "It's air cool. Rotary. It spin around in the air. It's much lighter, because it use-a no water."

The one in the straw boater turned to his friend and said, "It use-a no water! —You're wasting your time, Tommy. He's just a wop Italian. I'm going to the next tent."

But Tommy stayed, turned to Tito and spoke in carefully articulated French, saying, "Excusez! Où est le propriétaire de cet avion?"

Tito merely looked at him.

Aldo spoke up in French, saying, "I'm the owner. What's your question?"

"Thank you," the young man continued in French. "I like your aeroplane. I was wondering about the engine."

"The Gnome? It's fifty horsepower and it's air cooled, which means that we get a lot more power with a lot less weight."

Aldo was wearing a leather jacket over a thin sweater and his Zeiss goggles hung below his throat — gear from his automobile racing days.

"You're the flyer?" the young man asked, delighted.

"Yes."

"Is this a Voisin machine?"

"No, no. It's a Vela. I designed it."

"In France?"

Aldo smiled broadly and said, honestly, "Yes."

The young man — thin nose, spot of color on each cheek, flax hair — asked if it was difficult to learn to fly. Aldo told him it was no more difficult than learning to drive an automobile. The man, hands in his jacket pockets, peered into the cockpit a few moments, then walked slowly around the aeroplane, looking at it attentively. He asked Aldo a few more questions, smiled, said, "Merci beaucoup," and walked away. Aldo turned to Tito and said in Italian, "If that one comes back again, bring him to me. He's interested."

The Harvard-Boston Aero Meet went broke, but it was a success for most of the flyers and all the spectators, including circumferential president William Howard Taft, even though he was too heavy to be lifted an inch off the ground by any of the flying machines. The Englishman Claude Grahame-White won a lot of prizes, took mayor John Fitzgerald for a flight over Boston harbor, and made a little extra cash by charging passengers $500 for a fifteen-minute ride. Another Englishman named Roe made a flight in a machine that had three wings in a stack, but it crashed. Wilbur Wright came with his team, partly to fly and partly to keep his chill eyes on Glen Curtiss, whom he was suing. Aldo talked with other pilots, among them Charlie Willard, who was said to have graduated from Harvard, but who was for sure a former race car driver. And he had a good time with Didier Masson who had been a mechanic for Aldo's friend Paulham and who was now flying every chance he got. On the last day of the meet the pilots organized an egg dropping contest, the only contest Aldo enjoyed. He relished making turns and shallow dives that mocked the maneuvers he had watched a few days earlier when there had been a target battleship, reduced in size but true in shape, and flying machines had successfully attacked it with plaster bombs, thrilling government observers. "Bravo!" Aldo had said. "What happens when the target shoots back?"

"If there had been a prize for the most beautiful aeroplane," Molly told him. "We would have won it."

"Yes, we could have won it," he said, pleased that Molly had said we.

Thomas Pickering, the man who questioned Aldo about his flying machine, had returned two days later with a different friend. Pickering hailed Aldo in French, asking permission to show his friend "cet avion magnifique," and of course Aldo agreed, replying in French. During Pickering's previous visit Aldo realized that Pickering would be more interested in doing business if he believed Aldo wasn't Italian but French. Pickering and his friend, a man named Adams, examined the aircraft, were obviously fascinated and asked one question after another. Aldo's French was more fluent than Pickering's and as they wound up the conversation Pickering asked what part of France he was from. "Nice, near Italy," Aldo announced. "In fact, I raced automobiles in Torino, in Italy, before I designed aeroplanes. My mechanic is an Italian, a very good man."

The next month Aldo began to give flying lessons to Pickering at the farmer's field in Lexington, sailing over the scarlet sumac and yellow birches into the spotless air, into wide sweeping curves and lazy figure eights, doing the maneuvers again and again, at last returning down a long shallow slope to land on the straw colored field. After two days Aldo felt comfortable enough with his student to switch to English. "Your English is very good," Pickering exclaimed. "And — do you know? — you have an *Irish* accent!" Pickering turned up one afternoon with two friends, Norman Prince and Chad Washburn, both of them interested in aeroplanes and both astonished that Pickering was taking flying lessons. The first Vela aeroplane was purchased for $4,150 in November, 1910, by Thomas Pickering of Duxbury, Massachusetts. Chad Washburn purchased the next one, and after that the orders came flying in one after the other, came in flocks, to the Vela Aeroplane Company.

* * * * *

Sunday morning and they're boldly, bravely naked, those two. "We're going to be rich," Aldo announced, stretching back on the bed, folding his hands behind his head.

"For sure," said Molly, brushing her hair at the mirror. "We'll not be able to shut the dresser drawers, they'll be so stuffed with money."

Aldo laughed, swung his legs off the bed and stood up. "Maybe not that rich."

"Rich enough to eat ice cream every day?" she asked.

Aldo had drawn aside the window shade and was peering at the clear blue sky. "Yes, that rich."

"Let's put on our Sunday best and get our ice cream," she said, pulling a slip from the dresser. "Before the money's gone."

They got into their Sunday best, took the trolley

and subway to the Café Mondello. Molly looked around at the gold flocked wallpaper, the bright spacious mirrors, the gas chandeliers with electric bulbs. "I feel rich already," she said. "Like one of those grand horizontals in Paris." Aldo, unfolding his newspaper, murmured that this was a respectable Italian café and not a French bordello, and only the puritanical Irish would confuse the two. He scanned the headlines of *La Notizia*, folded the paper and put it aside. "My father would have liked this newspaper. Very socialist." Molly, who had been watching the family (mother, father, little boy) at the next table, smiled and turned to Aldo. "You loved your father," she said.

"Of course. Everyone who knew him loved him. Especially my mother. My father was a wonderful man."

"I loved my mother. I can say that." She spoke slowly, as if meditating. "But I cannot say I loved my father. Sometimes I felt sorry for him and a lot of the time I feared him. I just tried to stay out of his way. He had terrible rages, the old man. But your father was a gentle person."

"He liked people," Aldo said. "Above all, he loved my mother and me. He was a poet, you know. He was a journalist, of course, and a teacher, but at heart he was a poet."

"It must have been hard for you, a young boy, to lose — I mean — when he died —"

But Aldo cut her off, saying, "They beat my father to death! They broke his bones. They broke his head. If my father had a thought when he was dying it was to take care of us, of me and my mother. I couldn't protect him, but at least when I grew up I could avenge him."

Molly opened her mouth to speak, then stopped. "A poet," was all she said.

The waiter greeted them in Italian, briskly swabbed the small marble table top, took their order and dashed off.

"My father wrote a long poem about Daedalus and Icarus in Sicilian," Aldo told her. "He never finished it because he kept changing it. —You know the story of Daedalus and Icarus?"

"Not I."

"You were taught it in school, but you've forgotten it." He looked surprised. "It's about flying and —"

"Do you know Saint Patrick who drove the snakes out of Ireland? Do you know Saint Brendan who sailed to America in a stone boat?"

"No," he admitted.

"All right then," she said, satisfied. "Now you can tell me."

"It happened like this. It happened that Daedalus and his son Icarus escaped from an island prison by making wings from the feathers of sea birds. The old man was clever. He was famous for that. They glued the feathers together with bees' wax to make wings. Daedalus warned his son not to fly near the sun because it would melt the wax and his wings would come apart. But his son was enchanted by flying, drunk on flying — I can understand that, I feel

132

the same way myself — and he flew too close to the sun. The heat of the sun melted the wax, the feathers tore off, he fell out of the sky and into the sea and drowned. That's not the end."

"I don't like the way this story is going, Aldo."

"Neither did my father. In the old story Daedalus couldn't rescue his son, so he flew on and discovered Sicily. —It's a Greek story, and the Greeks think they discovered Sicily, even though we were already there. — My father didn't believe a father would watch his son struggling in the sea and not rescue him. He revised and rewrote that part over and over again."

"It sounds like an Irish poem, I'm sorry to say. Such grief."

"In my father's last version, Daedalus swoops low over the waves so Icarus can grab his father's ankles and he holds on as his father pulls him from the sea. His father uses all the strength in his old arms to beat his wings, lifting him just above the waves and over the sea to the shore of Sicily. Sometimes his tired wings touch the water, he was so —, but he —" Aldo's eyes had begun to glisten and his voice wavered. He dried his eyes and laughed. "So. Anyway. In my father's version, Daedalus tells his son to change his name and he, Daedalus, will tell everyone that his son is dead, drowned in the sea. That way, the cruel and stupid king who imprisoned them will not bother to send thugs to hunt Icarus down, and Daedalus is so old and in such grief that the king won't bother with him either. They were political prisoners, you might say, and Daedalus made up the story of his son's drowning in order to save him. Now you know the story of Daedalus and Icarus, the true version."

The waiter swept in with their spumoni — heaps of pastel hues, like frozen flowers in crystal dishes.

"Now *this* is spumoni. You will never find finer ice cream than this," Aldo told Molly.

They decided to move to a new flat, a bigger place. "Because, Aldo, this apartment has gotten so tight I have to leave my shadow outside when I come in."

"I was going to suggest a move," he said.

So in May of 1911 Aldo and Molly left the Fort Pont Channel place and moved to a larger third-floor flat in the West End, a neighborhood of Irish and Italians. "Ah, this is big enough to swing a cat in!" Molly said. Aldo was selling his aeroplanes, giving flying lessons, putting money away and feeling prosperous. Their landlord lived on the first floor, a veteran of the War Between the States (28th Massachusetts, part of the Irish Brigade) who had fought at Gettysburg and been wounded in the slaughter at the Wheat Field. He despised Republicans, especially Theodore Roosevelt. "That braggart loves playing at war. He loved playing war with Spain. Oh, yes. Him and his cavalry. He thinks it's a sport. He hasn't seen men die by the tens of thousands. I've seen it. I was there." Aldo doubted that men had died by the tens of thousands at Gettysburg, but he was polite. "That was a large war, the war between the states," he ventured.

"Jaesus, Mary and Joseph, it wasn't no sport!"

"We will have no more wars," Aldo said decisively, handing him the envelope with the rent money.

"Thank you. —And they weren't all dead, either. They were dying and it took all day. Oh, yes. But who wants to remember? Even I forget. And that's the truth. —I need to go pee."

There was a ghost, a young Irish woman in a moss-green head shawl, who sometimes appeared early in the morning seated on a step at the second floor. You could see her by looking up from the foot of the stairs or looking down slantwise from the third floor, but as you walked up or down the stairs your view was cut off at the turning of the staircase and when you reached the second floor she had vanished. Almost always she had vanished, but sometimes you had to step around her.

"How can you believe such things?" Pacifico asked, refilling her glass.

"Such things?" Molly said. "Would you be asking can I believe in a man whose hind end is the back half of a horse? Or a goddess who makes her bed in a whore house? Would you be asking me that?"

Pacifico gave a roar of laughter and slapped the table top in approval. "If you ever got to talk with this ghost, what would you say?" he asked, leaning slightly forward.

"I'd say, *In God's name what do you want.* That's the way you speak to haunts. You always begin with *In God's name.*" She tossed back her head, drank the last of her wine, banged her glass back on the table.

135

"That's what I was taught."

"The Irish converse with the dead," Aldo told Marianna. "They have grand funeral parties, too. We went to an Irish wake — an uncle of Molly's friend Kate had died — and it was like nothing in Italy or Sicily. They drink whiskey like it was mother's milk. Have you noticed all the funeral parlors in Boston are owned by the Irish? They open funeral houses the way we open restaurants. If you want to know anything about the dead, ask the Irish."

When Aldo paid the next month's rent he asked about the ghost. "Oh," his landlord said, brushing aside the question with a wave of his hand. "She's no banshee if that's what you're worried about."

That evening Aldo asked Molly what a banshee was.

"You've been listening to the Irish Brigade, have you? A banshee is a woman spirit who foretells a death in the family."

"Did the nuns teach you that or did you learn it with your accounting?"

"I know it because I'm an O'Neill. The banshee works only for the O'Neills, and the O'Briens, O'Connors, O'Gradys and Kavanaghs." She laughed. "I thought everyone knew that."

"What happens if a Miss O'Neill has married a Mr Vela from Sicily? Does the banshee still work for the former Miss O'Neill?"

"We don't know yet."

13

THE VELA AEROPLANE COMPANY moved closer to the West End where the owner himself worked full time and Tito half-time, along with a handful of employees, building aircraft. Over the next few years Aldo improved his aeroplane (landing gear, engine) but it remained essentially the same craft. It was beautiful to look at, easy to handle and graceful in flight. It took to the air readily and flew slowly. Yes, slowly — Aldo had designed it that way. Other aeroplanes flew faster and faster and faster. Speed wasn't important to Aldo, quite the contrary. Speed meant flying in a straight line from here to there, pausing to look at nothing, but he wanted to lazily meander, to circle the four-sided clock on the train station tower, climb higher into the sky, or drift low over the tall grasses that leaned with the flow at the river's edge. "This is a fair-weather aeroplane," Aldo used to say. "It's made to carry a couple to a picnic in the country, not to carry important mail or bombs. It's an aeroplane for holidays or romances and adventure." One of his improvements was a wicker basket, attached to the fuselage, to hold lunch and a bottle of wine.

In 1913 he designed his "Dragonfly" aeroplane, a ship somewhat similar to Louis Bleriot's second

1907 machine. It had two sets of wings, one pair behind the other, and a long tail. The design was prompted not by a wish to imitate Bleriot, but by Aldo's desire to reproduce the seemingly weightless beauty of nature's dragonfly. The aeroplane's wings were clothed with glittering translucent silk, and it flew well enough, but it remained a curiosity and sold only three copies. On the other hand, the basic Vela aeroplane sold very well. The wood frame was sheathed with plain linen which gave it a light dun or golden hue, but fancier models with cushioned seats had wings as gorgeous as orioles, tanagers or jays. For half a dozen years it was the most familiar aeroplane in all New England, New York and Pennsylvania.

Molly learned all she could about aerodynamics and gathered every number she could — all to keep Aldo from falling from the sky. She read books from the library and articles in *Aero,* but having gathered all the numbers there seemed no way to balance accounts, no established theory of flight, only a multitude of facts. Everyone knew that the curvature of the wings, the convexity of the upper surface — what the French called *cambrure* — was essential, but no one knew how much of a curve to make. She had read someplace that a propeller was simply a rotating wing, an idea that surprised and pleased her so much that she laughed out loud. A skimpy handful of people built wind tunnels to test their theories; everyone else built aeroplanes and flew them to see what would happen. Pilots crashed all the time, many got killed and no one worried. But Molly worried and in her nightmare an aeroplane lighted up the sky, plunging to earth like a meteor trailing fire.

"All life is risky, uncertain," Aldo said.

"But numbers are certain," she told him.

Flying delighted her just as Aldo had said it would. She felt there was a whimsy to it that no one had ever remarked upon. As for Aldo, she could tell he felt much more than delight — flying exhilarated him, the expansiveness of the view enlarged his soul and charged his intelligence. When others flew they were carried aloft in a flying machine, but when Aldo flew, he was the one flying and the machine was mere ballast — his feet on the rudder bar and his hands on the lever were sensate parts of the aeroplane, just as the wires stretching to the fuselage and wings were spliced to the coils of his brain. He was a man with wings. Given the chance, he would turn somersaults in the sky and hobnob with angels and gods. Before she met Aldo she had never feared because she had nothing to lose, but now she saw how she could lose everything.

Pacifico's wife Marianna had elegantly shaped breasts tipped with large rose nipples that were ever overflowing with sweet milk, and it seemed there was always a child suckling. Now she was breast feeding Dante, her fifth — or possibly Sandro, her sixth — handsome boys with thick black hair and eyes that glistened like fresh ink. Marianna was a smart, good looking, fertile woman. Maybe that's why one morning Molly told Aldo, abruptly, "My monthlies are as regular as the tides."

Aldo hesitated, his coffee cup half way to his mouth. "Your monthlies?"

"The bloody curse that God —"

"Ah! I understand," he said, nodding yes, slowly lowering his cup into its saucer. "I understand."

"Do you understand you will never have any children?"

"What do you mean?" he says, startled.

"I mean I got an abortion in Dublin when I was seventeen."

"Oh? *Oh!* God. Well. I don't —"

"If you thought you were marrying a virgin," she says tartly, "I'm sorry to disappoint you."

"What?" he says, looking at her, puzzled. "What!" he cries, reaching across the table to grab the throat of her shirtwaist, yanking her to her feet. *"Don't talk that way to me! Don't talk that way to me ever again! Understand?"* And he flings her back into her chair so hard it slides back a foot.

"Holy Mother of God!" she cries, whirling up and turning on him. "I have a past, you know!"

"Exactly! A past. That is *past.*"

"I'm me — past, present and future!"

"Be calm," he tells her. "Sit down. Be calm."

"And who are you to teach me that?" she says, and

snatching up the first thing she can get her hand on she hurls a wet dishrag at him.

Aldo caught the rag, quietly mopped the spilled coffee, rinsed the dishrag in the sink, squeezed it and hung it over the hook. "Tell me more," he said.

She sat down and gave half a laugh. "At the time I felt so relieved and free and happy and I thought — *so there is a God after all and he loves me.* I was happy, so happy. Now I think I'm cursed."

"No, no, no curse on you," he muttered.

"I murdered an innocent. I'm barren and it's my —"

But Aldo reached slowly across the table and put his hand to her mouth, stopping her.

"This is not the Dark Ages," he told her. "There's no more curses. I married you because of you, not because to have children. Yes," he added a moment later, as if discovering that he agreed with himself. "That's true."

"I murdered —"

"Molly, Molly. Listen to me." He put his hands flat on his chest. "I'll tell you what murder is. Murder is when you beat a man to death because you don't like his opinions. My mother and I, we moved from Sicily to Italy, to the north, far away to the north, to Torino. You know that. And before we left Palermo, my mother pointed out to me the house where lived the man who made my father to be beaten senseless and thrown into a filthy cell to die. I told you that, too. What I didn't tell you was that when I was a student at the engineering school in Torino I took a trip to Roma and from there to Napoli and from there I sailed to Palermo. I carried five wine bottles — very good looking wine bottles — filled with gasoline. In Palermo I walked down the avenue where my mother had pointed to the villa. It had looked like a prison castle when I was a kid, but it was only a bourgeois villa with a tile roof and some ugly wrought-iron growing over the ground floor windows. I strolled in the park along that avenue and asked who lives in that villa over there, and they told me, and it was the same man. That night I did what I had come to do, and the next morning I sailed from Palermo to Napoli and so back to Torino.

A month later my mother calls me into her room where she is standing beside her writing desk with a letter in her hand. She had received the letter from one of her socialist friends in Palermo describing how a certain villa had burned to the ground and everything in it was ashes. The man lived, but with many shattered bones because he ran in the smoke and fell down the stairs. Somebody had even shot the horse dead when it was pulling the carriage through the gate.

My mother asked me if I had been to Palermo. I said yes. She didn't say anything for a long moment, then she says, *You know the army and the police are everywhere. You could have been taken for a revolutionary. If anything happened to you I would die. Do you understand? Now promise me you will never go to Sicily again.* I promised. Then she kissed me on my cheeks, here and here, and she embraced me for a

142

long time.

That man with all the broken bones, he never got well. He died in pain." Aldo poured more coffee into his cup and lifted it, saying, "And — you see? — my hand doesn't tremble." He took a drink and set the cup neatly in its saucer.

"I should like to meet your mother some day," Molly said.

Aldo and his mother exchanged letters every month or so — short but gossipy letters about her daily routine, local politics, a wedding party or a funeral, the ailments of friends, the birth of children, certain opera singers, and so on. In August of 1914 he received a different kind of letter from Morgana. She was writing, she said, a day after learning that Jean Juarès, the great French socialist, had been gunned down in Paris by a crazed assassin. She admired Juarès, not simply because he was a socialist — the world had many kinds of socialists — but because he was wise, compassionate, peace loving, brave, resourceful and persevering. Sometimes it was difficult to realize that such people lived among us. Juarès had seen how monarchs and ministers were maneuvering, preparing their countries for war, and he had warned against such foolishness. He knew that hush-hush meetings and secret compacts guaranteed not peace but vengeance. He knew that if war came, ordinary people who wanted only to marry, to have a job and a family, would be sent to battle others like themselves. The murder of Juarès was a signal that a great war was about to begin. Her own mother used to say the gods employed death of a gallant man that way, as a sign their entertainment was about to start, like dimming the houselights before the opera curtain rises. She reminded Aldo that she was a pacifist, and she hoped, pleaded and begged he would not join in the fighting. The world was going to soak in blood. She told him to take care of his wife — *Stay by her side because the war will make her conceive and she will need you all the more.* — but if he ever did cross the Atlantic his mother would be waiting in Torino to embrace him and cover his cheeks with kisses.

As a matter of fact, on June 28, Austrian Archduke Francis Ferdinand and his wife had been assassinated in Sarajevo by a Serbian nationalist and, using that as a let's-pretend pretext, Austria-Hungary declared war on Serbia, after which Russia — allied with Serbia — began to mobilize against Austria-Hungary. These old wars are hard to keep straight and easy to forget, so here's the way it happened. On August 1, as Morgana was writing her letter to Aldo, Germany declared war on Russia, and two days later Germany also declared war on France. On August 4 Britain declared war on Germany. On August 6 Austria-Hungary declared war on Russia and on the same day Serbia declared war on Germany. On August 11 France declared war on Austria-Hungary and was joined the next day by Britain. Other nations, too numerous to remember, got in on the war. The following year, on April 26, 1915, Italy joined Britain and France against the Central Powers, and two years later on April 6, 1917, the United States declared war on Germany. By mid June, Aldo had arrived in France and was on his way to Tours, southwest of Paris, to train American pilots at the flight school.

Aldo had closed the Vela Aeroplane factory and Molly had begun working for the city of Boston, a job she got through Kate McCarthy who had connections to the ward boss under the mayor, James Michael Curley. Aldo left Boston near the end of May and Molly, despite her monthlies having been as regular as the tides, had no menstrual flow, though it should have come right then, nor did it come in June, not a drop of blood. She was writing one or two or even three letters a week to Aldo, but she never mentioned what had happened, or had not happened, because what it seemed to mean seemed impossible. Then one morning as she was descending the stairway on her way to work a wave of nausea lifted her stomach, made her dizzy, and she had to hold the rail all the way from the second floor landing to the front door.

Three nights later she wrote *Dearest Aldo, who I love more than ever you will be as amazed as I am for I am pregnant and we are going to have a baby. I went to Dr. White. And I talked with an old midwife from county Tyrone, my mother's own county, and the old woman asked me the same questions as Dr. White & few more personal as well. — Marianna calls it a joyful miracle and Maureen says it's like the barren woman in the Bible who gives birth when she's a hundred years old, or some such age. Maureen has a good heart but the Bible never did me any good & frankly now that I'm carrying a baby I'd sooner cross the street than be on the same side as a priest.*

Marianna and Pacifico have invited me to live with them, but I'm fine here in Boston, especially as it is so convenient to walk to work. Not that Marianna would notice one more baby among the eight or nine she has or will have when my time comes. I miss you more than ever I know you have to be over there. I know the Italians and Irish will never agree about this war, except that it is terrible. I miss you so much. Aldo Aldo. I write Aldo Aldo because I remember how you say Molly Molly when you want to tell me something. Now I have told you my news. Love, Molly.

As soon as Aldo read Molly's letter he dashed off a note to her, writing that her news made him happier than he could express, especially in English. *I feel as if I am filled up and overflowing. I am so happy as the day we married, which will always be the happiest day of my life. The war cannot go on forever and now that the United States is sending troops the war will soon be finished. I'll be home before our baby is born.*

He wrote again that evening, urging her to visit the doctor often and maybe visit Marianna's doctor and to move in with Marianna and Pacifico out-

146

side the city before the baby came. He wrote that he was getting acquainted with routine at the base. The French were generous and were delighted that the Americans were arriving in France. The newspapers had reported about the American infantry battalion marching in Paris on the 4th of July and how one of the officers had said "Nous voilà, Lafayette!" and the crowds of French had gone crazy with joy.

The young American pilots here for training are idealistic and enthusiastic but — the remainder of the sentence was blacked out by the French censor. *The aeroplanes we use for training are* — this part was blacked out — *with clipped wings. They clip the wings so the aeroplane can't take off. The student pilots run the machine up and down the field and learn the controls, but the poor plane is like a baby bird that flaps and flaps but can never fly.*

My head is full of thoughts of you and the baby. Do you think the baby will be a flier? I'm sure of it. Boy or girl, it makes no difference, nowadays women are fliers too. It will be wonderful.

Molly had never disagreed with Aldo; that is, she'd never disagreed profoundly. True, she'd had arguments with him and at times raged against him, cursed him, thrown things at him — a thin book, say, or a medium size dish, absolutely no knives — and in a burst of anger had once locked the bedroom door against him, which led to his kicking it open with the heel of his shoe, hurling the door around so hard the knob punched a hole in the wall, but nothing you'd call a *profound* disagreement. Yet ever since that let-

147

ter in which he said her baby would fly an aeroplane Molly had felt a deep and fearful disagreement with Aldo, and it was growing much like the infant in her womb. She would not have her child fall from the sky like one of those angels God threw over the edge. Her child would never fall flaming from the sky because she'd never let her child fly up there.

In mid-December one morning as she started down the stairway she was startled to see the ghost on the second floor landing. While Molly descended her view was cut off by the turn of the stairway, but when she reached the landing the specter was still there, sitting hunched on the step in a moss-green head shawl. Molly pulled the skirts of her coat aside to keep it from brushing against the specter, held her breath while she stepped carefully around it and, struggling to keep her balance, clutched the rail and made her way down to the door and out to the freezing rain. She didn't tell anyone what she had seen and she didn't write to Aldo about it. The next morning when she left the apartment she spied the apparition again sitting on the step at the second floor landing and nearly pitched headlong down the stairway. She grabbed the rail, descended to the second-floor, drew in her coat so as to not brush against the thing, whatever it was, and made a falling run down the stairs and out to the frozen street. "No, damnit!" she said. Then she turned around, yanked open the front door and lumbered up the stairs (she was 30 weeks pregnant, remember) to the second floor landing which was utterly vacant. She stamped down the stairs, muttering *Damn* at every step until she was out the door. Then she went off to work.

Molly wrote to Aldo that night, telling him about the apparition, but phrasing it in a playful way so he would not think she was wholly daft — yet informing him about it all the same — then taking it back at the end by saying the spirit was so solid looking it must have been real, no ghost, just some poor biddy taking refuge from the freezing cold weather. Knowing that Aldo would worry about her health and sanity and would think she was seeing weird things because she was living alone, she added that she'd already arranged to stay with the Cavallùs out in Malden. That Saturday she visited Pacifico in his corner office over the new store and — presto! — Molly agreed that she would take the train the day before Christmas and would stay with them until well after the birth of her baby. "Brava, Molly!" Pacifico said. "Marianna will be delighted to have company. Two babies will be twice more fun than one. I'll call doctor Balboni! —And I'll send a note to Aldo to tell him the good news."

"Oh, no. Let me," said Molly.

On February 25, 1918, around four in the morning, Molly was awakened, or half-awakened, by crying. The sound seemed composed not of one voice, but of many women's voices blended together, wailing and keening — something like wind shrieking at the edge of a door or like a woman in anguish. Molly lay listening to the sound and thought it strange that Marianna was not coming down the hall to comfort whichever child it was. She pushed aside the bed-clothes and walked down the dim hall toward the crying which was softer now, more like a moan, and glancing down the stairway saw the woman in the moss-green head shawl seated on the second step down, for it was she who was voicing grief. Molly bent down and whispered at her ear, "Go fuck off," then straightened and stepped into the bathroom. She picked up the first thing to hand, which was a tin cup half filled with water, turned and emptied it over the banshee — if that's what it was or had been, for it was gone now. Molly returned the cup to the sink and had started to walk back down the hall when the first contraction came, making her reach to the wall for support, squeezing her till she gasped.

Marianna had heard no wailing. But she did hear Molly cry out, so she shook Pacifico awake, then she stepped out to the hall and nearly bumped into Molly who, as Marianna always said, had been awakened by contractions and whose waters had now broken.

It was late in the afternoon when Brendan Neil Orlando Vela was delivered, covered with blood but safe, into this world. As for Molly, she lay in an exhausted stupor, awake without thought, feeling her body adrift on a gentle tide of air, or maybe it was only life ebbing away from her, she didn't know which. They brought the infant and laid it between her arm and her breast, and later they took it away. She slept, too tired even to dream. Late the next day she wrote a note to Aldo, simply the date and *My dearest Aldo, we have a son, a family. Love from your*

Molly.

By the time the letter had crossed the Atlantic and traveled to his base at Tours, Aldo was in Issoudun. He had been directed to deliver a Nieuport aeroplane to Issoudun where a group of pilots from the United States was being trained. The French had been flying Nieuports but were now flying the faster, more robust Spads, and were giving the old Nieuports to the Americans who had no planes of their own. Early in the morning of February 26 Aldo took off from Tours and flew toward Issoudun, climbing steadily while the land beneath him spread farther and farther like a blue expanding map. Somewhere near Issoudun a feather of flame blew from the engine, curled up and blew away, then another and another, much like feathers torn from the engine cowl. Instinctively he shoved the stick and sent the plane into a long plunge toward the earth. The allies had no parachutes and there was no way a pilot could escape from a fiery plane except by jumping to his death. A radiant burst of flame reached toward him from the engine, flowed over the arm he lifted to protect his face, curled along side his cheek and neck, lingering to set his flesh afire — then it was gone, as if he had driven out of reach. There came a huge CRACK sound as a slice of fabric tore from his wing, he pulled up, leveled the Nieuport, saw the broad field of the Issoudun aerodrome ahead and everything was strangely quiet and soft, as if he were falling asleep. That's about all he was able to recall. The Nieuport made a smooth landing and even before it had rolled to a stop three men had rushed onto the field and pulled him from the cockpit.

Aldo's mother, Morgana, made her way from Torino to Issoudun, took a room in a hotel. By the time she arrived he was out of danger, was free to walk the hospital grounds, and was thoroughly familiar with the extent of his disfigurement. Fire had eaten the flesh along his left forearm and hand, damaging the nerves to his fingers; he was receiving painful physical therapy for his hand. His left eye was blind. His left cheek, ear and neck had also burned, and much of the flesh of his ear had had to be surgically removed. As the seared flesh healed it took on a blotchy, mottled appearance and it tightened, tugging his lips on that side into a grimace. He talked about the war, about Molly and his son, about one thing or another, but not about the mess of his face, not until the day his mother was about to leave for Italy. They were at the train station, standing side by side on the platform, sheltered from the falling rain. "I want to meet your Molly someday," Morgana said. "You should bring her to Italy as soon as this war is over. I'm sure I'll like her. And I want to see my grandson."

Aldo burst out, "*My face will frighten my son, my own face — it will give him nightmares!*"

For a long moment Morgana remained as she was, gazing at the railroad tracks that gleamed in the rain. "Would you take your father back from the dead if his face was burned like yours?" she asked, not turning to him.

152

"Yes," he said. "Of course."

"Your son —"

"I know, I know," he said, not waiting for her to finish.

"This terrible war isn't going to last forever, and when it's over you can bring your family to Italy. — Now are you going to let me kiss you or not?"

* * * * *

So here they are one summer morning a year later, Aldo and Molly, loafing side-by-side on a rumpled sheet in the bedroom in their West End apartment, both of them naked as the day they were born. Or they were a moment ago. Now Molly has slipped into a wrapper and left the room, and Aldo has a towel around his waist and is at the bureau, putting on his eye patch. He lighted a cigar, one of those black twig-like Parodi cigars, and he was assessing himself in the bureau mirror when Molly came in carrying a tin tray with two cups of espresso. "I'm still in pretty good shape," Aldo announced.

"You figured that out, did you?"

"And there are many things to enjoy," he continued.

"Now what would you be thinking of?"

"This cigar. That espresso." He set down the cigar, lifted the little cup and took a drink. "Would you like me to sing *Molly Malone* for you?" He spoke in a thick brogue. "It's about a poor Irish lass, don't you know, a working girl."

"I married you to get away from all that. And you'll wake the baby."

Aldo smiled, though I have to admit the left side of his face remained in a grimace. "In Dublin's fair city," he sang. "Where the girls are so pretty —"

"I'll go get the baby," she said, stepping out to the hall. Aldo drained the little coffee cup and stretched out on the bed sheet. Molly returned a moment later with Brendan Neil Orlando Vela whom she laid on the bed between Aldo and herself. The baby squirmed around, got up on hands and knees and began climbing over Aldo's stomach, up his chest, into his face. They put him down again between them. "He's going to be an adventurer," Molly said, brooding. "He's going to live a life full of danger."

"That's all right. I protected him."

"When?"

"In France, when my plane caught fire. That was me, not him. So he's all right, safe and sound. I protected him forever."

"Forever?"

"Yes," he said. "Because I took the disaster."

"You can't say he won't have aeroplane disasters just because you did."

"I fooled the gods," Aldo said. "It was me who fell from the sky, not my son. The gods always want to kill sons, anyone's sons. I fooled the gods."

"That's not a logical argument, Aldo."

"You think the gods are logical? Oh, Molly, Molly.

The gods aren't logical. They're capricious, full of passion, ambition and rage."

"So are we. Does that make us godlike?"

"At our best," said Aldo. "Yes."

14

ALDO WAS RIGHT, HE HAD FOOLED THE GODS. In World War II his son Brendan, a fighter pilot, was shot down off the eastern coast of Sicily and survived without a scratch. Brendan flew with the 1st Fighter Group, the same unit to which Aldo had been flying that Nieuport in 1918. In 1943 the 1st Fighter Group flew P-38 Lightnings, a plane with an unusual design that delighted old Aldo. The P-38 had twin fuselages in parallel, with the pilot between them in a nacelle on the wing. It was a nimble fighter with four machine guns and a cannon, and it could climb skyward faster than any other aircraft, friend or foe. Brendan's squadron had completed a bombing run (15 July 1943) and was strafing targets of opportunity on the coastal road between Augusto and Catania. He came under ground fire, pulled up and was attacked by two ME-109s. He was climbing for the sun when his left engine exploded, shredding part of the wing and shattering his canopy. He unbuckled his seat belt, pulled the hatch release and was blown out of plane which began a long plunge earthward. Brendan fell from the sky while the glittering blue sea and the dun-colored land rolled this way and that beneath him. He pulled the rip cord, his chute opened and he landed on a quiet stretch of beach — so far as anyone can figure, it was the same quiet beach where Daedalus and Icarus had landed a few thousand years before.

Brendan was on his knees in the sand, hurriedly burying his chute and Mae West when a patrol of Italian soldiers turned up. He raised his hands and, speaking in Italian, said, "We're friends! Don't shoot!" The soldiers, scruffy and unshaven, held their rifles on him, looked him over. The sergeant asked where he was from, meaning what unit; Brendan, speaking in Italian, said he was from Boston. One of the soldiers asked Brendan if he knew a barber in Boston, his uncle, named Antonio Stella. Brendan explained that Boston was a big city and he couldn't know every barber but, he added, after the war he'd definitely look him up. The soldiers began arguing among themselves as to where they should take Brendan and then somebody remembered that they hadn't searched him for weapons, so the sergeant searched him and found he had only a pair of sunglasses, a pack of cigarettes and a Zippo lighter. The sergeant gave everything back to him. Brendan offered cigarettes all around; they lowered their rifles but declined the offer. "Where are the Germans?" Brendan asked. The sergeant sighed and looked tired. "Where are the British? Where are the Americans? And when will they get here? That's the real question." In the end Brendan was handed off to an Italian truck convoy going to Catania and from there was passed on to Messina where he was kept under guard in a small hotel with a group of other Allied officers. When the British and American troops entered the city, the guards surrendered to the prisoners, and Brendan rejoined the Twelfth Air Force.

Aldo had fooled the gods so well that even his godson was protected. Mercurio, Pacifico's son and Aldo's godson, was a gunner on a B-24 in the 98th bomb Group, Ninth Air Force. While returning from a raid on the rail yards in Rome (19 June 1943) the B-24 caught fire as they were approaching Palermo and everyone bailed out. The other's were never seen again, but Mercurio landed on the Via Imperatore Federico, ran up the street and vaulted over the wall into his father's garden. Three days later the US Seventh Army took Palermo and Mercurio linked up with his bomb group.

The Vela aeroplanes were already old fashioned when Aldo halted production in December of 1916. They were meticulously hand made and were certainly the most beautiful flying machines of their time, but by the end of the Great War Aldo's concept of a low leisurely flight over a slowly unrolling landscape — that was gone forever. In the 1920s he designed luxury aircraft for wealthy patrons who in an earlier era would have been content with yachts, and in 1933 he bought a Beech Model 17 "Staggerwing" plane and began a passenger-and-freight service, flying here and there across New England. His company survived the Great Depression and World War II and he had a fleet of four or five air-

159

craft when he sold out in 1953. Molly worked in progressive politics, sometimes in the local Democratic party, other times in more radical movements.

✳ ✳ ✳ ✳ ✳

I never noticed it at the time, but looking back I see they were a handsome couple. Molly had thick white hair, clipped somewhat short and brushed back. Aldo had had facial surgery in the 1920s which permitted him a more symmetrical smile, but when aroused to anger or laughter there was still a tug at the left corner of his mouth and an animal flash of teeth. We kids — this must have been in the late 30s — used to beg him to take out his glass eye, so as to frighten us and, when he did, we'd shout and run away — shocked, horrified, delighted. In his later years he preferred to go without his glass eye and to wear a black eyepatch.

Now let me show you three of those black-and-white photographs taken by Pacifico at the Harvard-Boston Aero Meet back there in 1910. This one shows a group lined up in front of Aldo's aeroplane — here, from left to right, are Enzo (bowler hat) with his two serene sisters, then Tito in blazing white shirtsleeves, Aldo and Molly and Molly's lively friend Kate and, at the farthest right, Pacifico's regal wife Marianna. This other one shows the Vela aeroplane viewed from the front left side, the convex upper surface of the wing quite noticeable. (The kid looking at the tail section is just a passerby, but — who knows? — if he's twelve he could be Nicolo Pellegrino who became an aeronautical engineer and married Pacifico's daughter Marissa in 1929.) This last photo is an unposed snapshot — Aldo wears a leather jacket with a scarf or long oil rag over his shoulder, and he's pushed his goggles up onto his forehead. He's turned toward Molly who has a hand on his arm and is saying something to him. The empty cockpit is visible to the right and you can make out the back of the pilot's chair made of woven cane. Molly died in 1961 at age seventy-four, Aldo in 1968 at eighty-two. You can fool the gods, but only for so long.

Everyone died. Louis Bleriot, whom Aldo admired for designing and enthusiastically test flying one machine after another until he finally got one to really go, died in 1936 at age sixty-four. Aldo's French friend, Louis Paulhan, who won prizes at the Los Angeles Air Meet in 1910, and who won the Daily Mail's £10,000 London-to-Manchester competition the same year, died in 1963 at age eighty. Claude Grahame-White, the good loser in the London-to-Manchester flight, won prizes at the Harvard-Boston Aero Meet and died in 1959 at age eighty. Charles Foster Willard, the Harvard graduate who raced cars and flew aeroplanes, that same Charlie Willard whom Aldo met at the Harvard-Boston Aero Meet, died in 1977 at age ninety-four. The West End landlord who fought at Gettysburg died around 1920 and was said to have been eighty years old. He was the one who had seen men die by the tens of thousands during three summer days in 1863.

15

Enzo Augusto Capellino — Enzo the tailor, the same Enzo who helped Aldo Vela stretch fabric over his aeroplane frames, *that* Enzo — invented something even more astonishing than a flying machine. It was used only once, and that was in Cambridge, Massachusetts, in May of 1928. All this happened because of Lydia Webster Chase — shy, tall, beautiful Lydia.

Lydia Chase was the daughter of Prescott Chase, a retired professor of botany at Harvard University. Enzo and Lydia knew of each other only because her father had his shirts and suits made in Capellino's shop. One day in 1908, while being fitted for a summer-weight linen suit jacket, Professor Chase happened to make small talk about gardening. Now, young Enzo Capellino was an avid gardener and he invited the professor to walk through the sunny patch he cultivated behind his shop. Old Professor Chase was delighted by this tangled paradise of Sicilian fruit trees, grapevines and vegetables, and in return he invited Mr Capellino to visit his garden, a half-acre of flower beds, cool moss and ferns and fish pools, gravel walks and willow trees which lay behind his large square house on Kirkland Street.

In the years that followed, the elderly professor

and the young tailor visited each other's gardens once every June, exchanging seeds and cuttings. A certain decorum clothed these visits, partly because Professor Chase had been taught to treat social inferiors with polite formality and partly because Mr Capellino had been taught to show deference to his elders, and the professor was clearly a generation older.

In May of 1927 the professor's daughter, Lydia Chase, visited the tailor's shop for the first time, bringing with her the measurements for her father's summer shirts. Enzo looked up from his cutting table that day and saw a tall, slender woman dressed in white, a beautiful woman with a distracted look about her. She moved with an elegant awkwardness, as if — as if — as if, he thought, she were a large-winged crane or snowy egret, a creature who would be superbly graceful the moment she took flight, for air would be her natural element, not earth. Enzo himself was so distracted by her that it was not until after she left that he looked at the measurements she had given him. He saw that they were much shrunken from a year ago.

Miss Chase returned to Mr Capellino's shop a few weeks later to pick up the shirts. Enzo understood from the terribly diminished measurements that the professor, her father, was very sick. He wanted to solace Miss Chase, who was clearly even more distracted than before, but found that all he could say was, "I hope Professor Chase is well." To which Lydia replied, "Thank you." She flushed slightly, hesitated as if to say something more, then turned and left the shop, bumping ever so slightly into the door on her way out.

* * * * *

Prescott Chase, Harvard Professor Emeritus of botany, veteran of the Civil War, died in December of 1927 at the age of eighty-four and was buried next to his wife and son in Mount Auburn Cemetery. Prescott's old friends had already died or were ailing and housebound, and Christ Church, though small, looked quite empty. Lydia's women friends attended the service, as did five of the professor's former students and the President of the Charles Downing Horticulture Society. After the service, as Lydia followed the coffin past the empty pews, she noticed a solitary man standing halfway to the back of the church. He was of medium height, or somewhat shorter, and he was gazing at her with enormously sad, sympathetic eyes. It was not until she was home and had closed the door behind her that Lydia remembered him as the tailor, Mr Capellino, upon which she suddenly burst into tears.

Lydia's friends visited her regularly that December, but by the last week of January, 1928, the only visitor she had was a librarian from Harvard who had asked to examine her father's books and papers to see if there was anything valuable she could give to the university. She was lonely.

The figure of Mr Capellino refused to abandon Lydia's memory, so in February she visited his shop. He was even shorter and darker than she had recalled, and the shop more cluttered. But when he stepped forward to greet her he smiled, his face lighting up so much at the sight of her that she forgot what she had planned to say and fumbled with pleasantries about the weather. As for the weather, sleet and freezing rain had kept everyone else at home, so the shop was empty. Lydia recovered herself and said she hoped Mr Capellino could help her choose a necktie as a gift. Enzo explained that he had no neckties.

"No neckties?" she echoed, glancing about with a worried look.

"Please make yourself comfortable, Miss Chase," he said. "I'll make tea."

Lydia sat in a chair beside the cutting table and removed her gloves. Enzo brought out a ceramic tea service whose brightly painted teapot was in the shape of a hen.

"My mother died many years ago and my father needed somebody, needed me, to take care of the house, take care of him and the house," Lydia blurted out, as if she had been asked.

"I understand," Enzo replied gently, pouring tea. "I was eighteen when my father died. I had to take over the shop to help my mother and to make dowries for my two younger sisters. My sisters married seventeen years ago, and my mother died three years ago, and here I am today."

166

Lydia nervously twisted her gloves in her lap and wondered what to say next. "You garden on summer evenings," she ventured.

"And I read on winter nights," Enzo said.

After a moment she asked, "Have you ever wished to escape time, Mr Capellino, so as to change your life?"

"Often," he said, looking up at her.

"Would you change things in the past or the future?"

"You cannot change the past, only the future," he said.

"Somebody should build a time machine to go to the future," Lydia said, smiling for the first time.

Enzo was enchanted by her smile. "I will do that," he told her.

One afternoon Enzo looked up from his jumbled cutting table and there was Lydia, standing tall in the middle of the shop. Snowflakes melting on her black cloche hat and on her long black coat gave her the appearance of — the appearance of — Yes! Enzo thought, the appearance of the night sky clothed with stars. She asked Mr Capellino for help in choosing a pair of gentleman's leather gloves. He explained that he didn't carry gloves. "No gloves?" Lydia said, looking about vaguely.

"No one will be coming here in this blizzard," Enzo said, quickly bringing out a painted coffee pot shaped like a rooster. "Please make yourself comfortable."

He was pouring coffee from the brightly colored pot when Lydia asked him, "Have you thought about the time machine?"

"I've thought about it for years."

"How would it work?" she asked.

"Einstein has written about the fabric of space-time," he began.

"Einstein? The fabric of space-time?"

Enzo set down the pot. "Those are his words, yes. And I wondered about this fabric. He said it was curved, and I know something about fitting pieces of flat fabric over a curved surface. And as I thought about it, evening after evening, I came to see that the past is like a tightly woven bolt of cloth, endlessly wide and endlessly long and endlessly deep."

"And the future?"

"The future is being woven in this passing instant, right now. When we say *now* we refer to the edge where the threads are being brought together. A time machine will permit us to get just ahead, just a wee bit ahead, just a thread's breadth ahead of now. And once there, we can weave life any whichway we want, to please ourselves." He had never felt so confident and he broke into a smile.

Lydia had discovered she deeply enjoyed talking this kind of nonsense with Mr Capellino. "And what would it take to leap the distance of one thread ahead of now?" she asked with a smile.

"A lightning bolt," he said, laughing for the delight he saw in her face.

Lydia stayed talking with Enzo rather longer than the last visit and enjoyed herself more than she had in a long time.

The next time Lydia and Enzo met, a gust of wind blew Lydia's umbrella inside out just as she came in the door. She was gasping for breath and her face was drenched with rain. Enzo produced a dazzling white handkerchief and dabbed gently at her cheeks, but after three dabs the couple became embarrassed at how close they were to each other. Abruptly Enzo busied himself in fixing her umbrella while Lydia composed herself. She asked did he have any books, and Enzo laughed and answered no, no books, only men's clothing.

"The man who came from Harvard is cataloging my father's library and putting *all* the books in order," she said, looking around as if seeing the shop for the first time. "He's very good at making things neat and orderly. Perhaps you could use —"

But Enzo interrupted to tell her, "They are like diamonds in your hair, those raindrops." That was the first time he had ever said anything like that, and he was as surprised as Lydia by his boldness. He went off and returned with a tray and two glasses. "A little sweet wine from before Prohibition," he explained.

Lydia sipped from her glass, coughed and put her hand to her chest as the wine went down. "How would one get a lightning bolt?" she asked.

"I'll make one."

"Is that possible?"

"Yes, certainly. Before my parents immigrated to this country they lived in Palermo and saw Augusto Righi demonstrate his lightning machine at the University. My father was very impressed by Righi. He saw the demonstration twice and told me about it many times. My middle name, Augusto, is after Augusto Righi."

"The machine made lightning bolts?" Lydia asked, beginning to smile.

"Little lightning bolts, yes. Or, as you might say, very large sparks." Enzo, too, began to smile.

"How would one make a time machine?"

"It's the same as with making a suit. First I make the pattern, then I make the finished suit — or in this case, the machine."

"But how does it work? I mean, how does lightning make the time machine possible?"

"The lightning bolt makes a tiny rip in the fabric of space-time, in the precise present, in the *now*. And if you are right there when it happens, as close as you can get, you will suddenly find yourself on the frayed edge of the fabric of space-time. It stands to reason."

Lydia felt unreasonably happy. "When the time is right, I would like very much to see your machine."

"I'll invite you."

Lydia stayed and talked with Enzo until he closed the shop and then she walked home, reflecting on all the turns their conversation had taken.

* * * * *

Augusto Righi (1850-1921) is probably best known for his study of electromagnetic oscillations. His principle teaching post was at the University of Bologna, but he also taught at the University of Palermo in the years 1880-1885. The machine which Enzo Capellino's father saw Righi demonstrate was most likely the one designed by Righi to accumulate weak electric charges. Essentially, the apparatus consisted of a rubber belt looped between two metal pulleys set one above the other, and at the upper end of the loop the belt traveled through a small opening into a hollow copper sphere, leaving its electric charge there. In theory, there is no limit to the voltage which can be accumulated on the sphere. Probably the earliest precursor of Righi's apparatus was a device built by Walckiers de St. Amand in France in 1784. His machine was simply a silken belt stretched between two rollers, so that when you turned the rollers the silk moved, rubbing against small cushions positioned at the rollers, thereby accumulating an electric charge.

Enzo had long known that if he brushed his hand across certain materials, such as fur or wool or silk, an electric charge accumulated, so that if he then reached for a piece of metal a spark would jump from his finger to the metal, giving him a tiny shock.

In his tailor shop he had noticed that he was able to get a particularly large spark by drawing wool cloth across the brass yardstick which formed the end of his cutting table, so he planned a machine with a broad continuous belt of thick wool looped tightly between two brass rollers and, of course, at one end there would be a large hollow copper sphere, pierced with a hole so that one of the rollers could be fixed inside.

✳ ✳ ✳ ✳ ✳

The sky was blue and the air warm when Lydia next visited the tailor's shop. The clothing dummy in the window — the top half of a cheerful man who had worn a Harris tweed jacket all winter — now wore a white jacket with bright azure stripes; furthermore, he had a straw boater on his head and his stiff hands were holding a cardboard sign (*On Vacation! Will return in future.*) The door was unlocked, so Lydia walked through the shop and out to the garden where Enzo, in his shirt sleeves, was bent over a gleaming brass roller at least a yard long. His back was toward her, so she called out, "Mr Capellino, hello." He straightened up and turned around, smiling. "You make my name sound so beautiful," he said. "Please call me Enzo."

"And you may call me Lydia, if you wish," she replied.

172

"Lydia, I'll get us something cool to drink." He dashed up a rickety flight of outdoor stairs and entered the floor above the shop. Lydia looked around at the curved sheets of metal which lay here and there, and at the tangled garden which was just beginning to come into blossom. Enzo returned with a painted tray bearing a bottle and two glasses half filled with ice.

"You are actually building an actual time machine," Lydia said, clearly surprised.

"Actually, yes." He poured something as dark as coffee from the bottle into one of the glasses and handed it to her.

"Now, I hope you will accept this," Lydia said, handing him a large flat parcel. While Enzo unfolded the wrapping paper, she told him, "The librarian from Harvard says that the bookcase behind my father's desk has a number of valuable books about botany and horticulture. Dwight — he's the librarian — knows about these things, about how valuable the books are. Right down to the penny. He said somebody might steal one of the volumes and he wants me to donate them to Harvard for permanent safekeeping. He's not interested in this one and he let me take it from the house. It's my father's garden diary, all about the flowers in back of our house. Twenty years of notes and drawings."

Enzo gently opened the worn volume. "This is wonderful, truly wonderful," he murmured. "It's a treasure, a treasure," he said, tenderly turning the pages. "I appreciate your thinking of me," — he was pressing the notebook to his chest as he said this — "but this valuable journal should remain in your family, in your hands," he said, giving it back to her. "Your father was a great botanist. He loved his plants almost as much as he loved you."

Lydia's eyes glistened and there was an awkward silence. Enzo raised his glass. "To you," he said cheerfully and he drank.

Lydia raised her glass. "To you," she echoed. The beverage was like liquid fire and not sweet. "*Well!*" she said, gasping from the drink. "Well, well, well. Please tell me about your machine."

Enzo described how he was building a hollow metal tube which would be about four feet in diameter and stand about twenty feet tall. Inside, at the bottom of the tube, was a brass roller driven by an electric motor. A broad belt of wool ran from the bottom roller, up the tube and over another brass roller, then down the tube to the bottom roller again. And at the top of the tube there would be a great hollow metal sphere to gather the electric charges which would fly from the cloth, he explained. "That's the hard part," he added.

"The electric charges?"

"No. The hard part is getting the sphere to rest just right at the top of the tube. It's already fallen down twice. I think I've misplaced some pieces."

"It's best to keep everything in its place, because then there's a place for everything. That's what Dwight says."

"Oh, yes. Dwight," murmured Enzo. "Would you

like a little more wine?"

"Is it legal to drink this?"

"Oh, yes. My father made this many, many years ago. Before Prohibition. He loved to make wine. Shall I refill your glass?"

Lydia, began to laugh — a remarkably rich musical laugh. "Ah, Enzo, please, do," she said, holding out her glass. She was, Enzo realized, just the slightest bit drunk. The days were getting longer and they enjoyed each other's company until twilight when Lydia said goodbye.

Under the hot sun Enzo had stripped to the waist and was working on the starter switch of the time machine when Lydia walked into the garden. "Hello, Enzo," she said. "I received your invitation and here I am." The 1920s fashion for women was all flatness and no curves, which struck Enzo as comically wrong, yet as she came walking in her sleeveless dress, one hand swinging the long strand of large green beads she wore around her neck, she was the most desirable woman in the world. As for Lydia, she wondered why she was there, saying hello to this short bronze man whose shoulders glistened with sweat and whose thick chest hair — well, Enzo had already snatched up his shirt and was buttoning it while she took in the great time machine. It stood

175

erect in the center of the small garden, a thick twenty-foot column topped by a sphere which had been beautifully proportioned to the shaft but, as Enzo explained to Lydia, it had fallen a few times and was now somewhat reshaped. Indeed, it resembled a blunt arrowhead pointing skyward. "What do you think?" Enzo asked her.

Lydia shaded her eyes with her hand and gazed up at his apparatus. "It reminds me of something. I can't think what. It's rather like — Oh! — It does look rather like a, or like the —" Lydia hesitated, searching for the proper term. "Yes, like a stamen, the stamen of a great flower."

Enzo stood beside her, also looking up at it. "Ah, I had not thought of that," Enzo said slowly. "But, yes, I suppose it does."

"And it will make lightning?" she asked him.

"Yes, at the top. I'm sure of that."

"And the lightning will tear the fabric of space time, make a little rip in it?"

"Yes, I'm sure of that, too."

"And you'll be able to leap forward into next year or the year after that?"

"Ah," Enzo sat down on a small garden bench. "I'm not so sure of that. I've been working without sleep for the past five days. But I hope so." Indeed, he did look tired.

"I hope so, too," Lydia said.

"I'll get us a cool drink," Enzo said. He went up the wobbly flight of outdoor stairs and into his rooms above the shop and came back down with a basket of ice which cradled two large bottles of wine and two glasses. The day was warm and there was an uncertain breeze that blew strongly one moment and vanished the next, leaving only a dry stillness. Lydia sat on a cast-iron garden chair and Enzo sat on the small wood bench and they drifted in a long winding conversation as they drank the cool wine.

Lydia asked him about the metalwork at the top of the outdoor stairway. "It looks like a big bird cage," she said.

"Ah, that's a protective cage," Enzo said. "After starting the machine, I'll go up those stairs and get inside it. At that height I'll be level with the top of the lightning machine and close to it, but the lattice of metal will protect me from being hit."

Lydia looked worried. "Are you sure you'll be safe? Won't you be electrocuted?"

Enzo smiled. "I'll be safe. My only worry is that the rip in the fabric of space-time won't be big enough for me to slip through."

Lydia looked at the metal column with its banged up arrow-head crown. "How strange," she said reflectively. "Here you are on an ordinary Monday afternoon. You're about to leap forward in time, and no one knows."

"You're here and that's the world to me. Now it's time I tested it." Enzo strode to the machine and pressed the starter button. The motor began turning the brass roller so the great wool belt began to move, rising up inside the tall metal cylinder, passing over the roller inside the metal sphere and down again.

Little by little the speed of the rollers increased, the belt blurred and the air was filled with a humming rattle. Enzo drank off the last of his wine, tossed the glass over his shoulder — he discovered that he could make these bold gestures with complete confidence so long as Lydia was nearby — and mounted the trembling stairway to the lattice cage. He stepped into the cage and looked down to the garden to discover that Lydia's chair was empty. She was running up the stairs. She called to him, but the humming of the machine had grown louder.

"The librarian is going to ask me to marry him," she said. "I don't know what to do. I haven't been able to sleep for days."

"I can't hear you," cried Enzo from inside the cage, plainly shocked at what he had heard.

"He wrote me a letter last week, saying he was going to ask me this evening."

"The librarian!"

"Yes, Dwight has a schedule and this evening he's going to ask me to marry him. What do you think —"

"I think he's an unpronounceable clump of consonants," Enzo shouted over the growing thunder of the machine.

"Dwight says the future is known to people who make schedules."

"Will you marry a man who has a place for everything and everything in its place? A time for everything and everything in its time?"

"I'm forty-one years old and no one has ever proposed marriage to me," she said, lifting her voice against the crackle of sparks.

"I'm forty-three and have never dared propose marriage to anyone. I've achieved nothing!"

A bluish glow hovered over the row of phonograph needles which were fixed a hairsbreadth from the flying surface of the belt and long thread-like sparks began to flare from the bent edges of the sphere atop the machine.

"You have made this wonderful machine," she cried. *"But it may work no better than I have!"*

Enzo threw open the lattice door and started out to meet her just as Lydia started in, the two clutching each other as the first lightning bolt unfurled and snapped overhead like a colossal whip. The hair on Enzo's chest burst into flame, scorching Lydia's breasts. The world overflowed with light as every nail and rivet, every garden tool, the cast iron garden chair and even the garden itself surged toward them, all the while flaring apart, coming undone. "Yes!" Lydia thought ·— or maybe she actually cried aloud — "Yes! We're at the front edge of *now* and these are the raveled threads of space-time." And everything melted like a meteor into the rising dark.

* * * * *

When Enzo opened his eyes he was flat on his back in the garden. He realized that his arms were around Lydia, her arms over his shoulders and her eyes closed in sleep. The collapsed remnants of the lattice cage lay upon them like a shredded blanket. Lydia opened her eyes and sat up. She looked at the blue sky, glanced down at her singed dress and the string of melted beads, then looked at Enzo. "We're alive and it's a beautiful day," she said. "Yes," said Enzo, looking at his pocket watch whose fused hands said three o'clock. "And I wonder *which* day it is." They went through the shop and out the front door to the street to ask the first passerby what day it was and what time of day. It was three in the afternoon on Tuesday, May 22, 1928, precisely twenty-four hours forward from where they had been. "You've worked wonders, Enzo. We've jumped a day ahead and we're free to make whatever we want of our time."

"I propose marriage," he said, smiling up at her.

"I accept," she said, returning his smile.

Then they set off to get dinner, because they both felt wonderfully hungry, quite famished in fact, as if they had been asleep and had not eaten for a whole day.

※ ※ ※ ※ ※

In June of 1928 a man buying a seersucker jacket asked Enzo what the equipment in the back yard was for. When Enzo told him that it was a machine for generating lightning bolts, the man became extraordinarily interested and asked so many questions that Enzo, in a burst of confidence, began to tell him about the fabric of space-time, upon which the man gave a short laugh and said the tailor didn't know what he was talking about.

In 1929, a year after Enzo and Lydia had made their jump forward in time, Robert Van de Graaff built a small electrostatic generator at Princeton University, capable of producing around eighty thousand volts. At the inaugural dinner of the American Institute of Physics, he demonstrated an improved version of the same apparatus. It resembled in all essentials the very much larger and more powerful machine which had stood behind Capellino's shop three years earlier. In 1931 Van de Graaff joined the Massachusetts Institute of Technology and began assembling a double generator composed of two twenty-three foot high columns each containing two belts and support-ing an aluminum sphere six feet in diameter. This machine, capable of generating 50 million electron volts, was housed in its own building at MIT and, after some changes, was used as an atom smasher. In the 1950s MIT donated it to the Boston Museum of Science and in 1980 the Museum installed it in the Thomson Theatre of Electricity where it currently produces spectacular demonstrations of man-made lightning.

* * * * *

Enzo and Lydia were married on Saturday, June 23, 1928, and their daughter, Abigail Santuzza Capellino, was born in autumn of the following year. They lived in the large square house on Kirkland Street, and Enzo continued to work as a tailor for some months, then sold his shop in order to devote himself to the extensive Chase gardens which were succumbing to overgrowth and weeds. Old Professor Chase's collection of works by Charles Downing led Enzo and Lydia to an interest in pomology, and they became quite expert in that field, publishing a number of papers on apple species of New England and New York.

Although they wrote for scholarly horticultural journals and for garden club magazines, neither Enzo nor Lydia ever published anything about their time transit. They remained silent about the event partly because they enjoyed their privacy, and partly because they came to know how dangerous the experiment had been. They were lucky to have awakened with nothing worse than hunger pangs, as if they had merely been asleep for a day, but they feared some other experimenter might not survive. Despite the protective metal latticework, technically known as a Faraday cage, the couple were fortunate not to have been electrocuted — much as Ben Franklin, flying his kite into an electrical storm, had been fortunate. Lydia and Enzo enjoyed taking their grandchildren to the Museum of Science in Boston to witness the lightning bolts thrown off by the electrostatic machine there, and a lightning flash during a summer storm always remained a happy sight for the couple. Enzo Augusto Capellino (1885-1970) and Lydia Prescott Capellino (1887-1971) escaped time for a day.

16

PACIFICO CAVALLÙ, son of young Fimi Cavallù and the mature, learned and passionate Sonia DiSecco, grandson of Angelo Cavallù (man from the waist up, stallion from the waist down) and seventeen-year-old Ava, that same Pacifico arrived in Boston in the early spring of 1902. Three weeks later he was in the frozen Maine woods, part of a crew hacking out a road for dray horses. The crew was made up of Sicilians, Calabrians and Neapolitans. The foreman was a Maine man named Nadeau, a drunk who knew a dozen words in Italian, enough to get the job started, but on the third morning he didn't appear. The workers were standing with their hands in their pockets by the ice-covered tool shed when a boss turned up and asked who among them spoke English. Pacifico said he spoke English. "Read that sign over there," the boss said. And Pacifico said, "Pelletier engineering and construct company. Abasolutely no drink on the —" And the boss cut him off, saying, "Fine. You're the new foreman."

After he had been on the job three months Pacifico's muscles were hard as rocks and the boss — his name was Bowman, you recall — called him aside, told him to come along to Boston to round up more Italian workers. "We're running out of Irish and this time of year the Frenchies quit to go work on their farms. We'll take the train tomorrow morning. Shave good and put on your white shirt." Three days later, on the train back from Boston, Bowman took out a roll of bills and peeled off an extra day's wages which he gave to Pacifico. Pacifico said, "Next time we go, you tell me ahead of time and I can have Italians lined up and waiting when we get there. Save you time."

Bowman smiled just a bit. "Maybe I like staying in the city for a couple of nights on company money," he said.

"Maybe you can stay in the city on company money and not to worry, because I will have a crew at the train station when you ready to go back," Pacifico told him.

"You can do that?"

Pacifico laughed. "Leave it to me," he said.

Pacifico went to the city with Bowman three times, acting as go-between each time. On their third and last trip Bowman paid him on the crowded sidewalk in Boston, as agreed. "I don't judge a man by his name," Bowman told him, handing him his wages.

"Neither do I," said Pacifico with a quick smile. "Any time you need workers, let me know. I'll have them waiting when you get here."

"Well," said Bowman. "I'll do that."

They shook hands, then Bowman shepherded the workers to the railroad station and Pacifico walked around the corner to Prince Street, to a general store where he'd lined up a job on his previous trip to Boston. The store — you remember this — was badly managed by a fretful Neapolitan who didn't speak English as well as Pacifico, so Pacifico's job was to cope with the American suppliers, talk to them, write business letters to them, and translate documents from the Shawmut Bank credit department. He also worked behind the counter and hauled barrels up from the cellar. Nine months later he made his first payment toward buying the business and that same night he wrote a letter to Marianna Moretti, telling her he was established now and they could marry as soon as she arrived. Marianna came down the gangway onto the snowy dock in Boston early in 1904.

According to Nick Pellegrino, the couple were married right there on the dock. Maybe it happened that way — their breath making cloudlets in the freezing air, the Justice of the Peace holding out a pen in one hand and in the other a marriage certificate, two customs officers as witnesses, blowing on their hands and stamping their feet to keep warm. But we all know Nick was told that story by his aunt Gina as they lay naked and sweaty on her sun filled bed, so maybe Nick wasn't listening attentively and got it wrong. Furthermore, the family's spoken history has always said that Marianna's mother came down the gangway one step behind her daughter, and that the couple married in a church. So Nick wasn't listening. Or maybe Gina *did* tell him that tale, but only because it's a common immigrant story and people like to hear it.

Or maybe it's true. Maybe Diva Moretti didn't

come down the gangway one step behind her daughter, didn't spend the next three weeks chatting with this old lady and that little girl throughout the North End to satisfy herself that Pacifico didn't already have a wife tucked away someplace. Maybe Diva didn't care if her daughter's marriage was attested to only by a scrap of paper signed by a faceless notary, and didn't care if there was no ceremony in Saint Leonard's church where the priest spoke Latin to God and Florentine to the parishioners. After all, Diva was the daughter of Stella DiMare, a goddess so beautiful her looks could stun, and half-divine Diva cared little about Jesus and even less about the Pope and his priests. But family history says they married in a church and that their signatures are on the registry at Saint Leonard's, or if not at Saint Leonard's then Saint Stephen's, or if not Saint Stephen's then certainly Sacred Heart, or in one of those other churches that long ago closed its doors and are gone from the North End.

Pacifico and his bride lived in the front half of a flat that was up a narrow flight of stairs (the bottom steps smelled of piss) off a littered alley from jam-packed Hanover Street. He enjoyed showing Marianna around the city. "All around here is called the North End," he told her. "Because it's the north end of Boston. If you go down any of these little streets you come to the ocean and fishing boats, just like Palermo — but with ice and snow." They threaded their way along the crowded sidewalk. "And everybody lives beside everybody else, the Irish there, the Jews along Salem Street, the Italians here." He laughed and put his arm around her waist. "That's the way it is in this country, everybody rubs shoulders with everybody else." As the weather warmed they walked farther into the city and he pointed out the Customs House tower, took a ride on the underground train, went into the gold domed State House, admired the sacred Cod Fish ("In the beginning they were fishermen, like your father's family," he explained.) then Boston Common and — now that it was spring — the Public Gardens with its tranquil pond and slow gliding swan boats. As they turned homeward they passed through noisy North Square. "This is where I was hired for my first job. And this is where I gather the workers for Mr Bowman to go to Maine."

"Why are they taking the top off that building?" Marianna asked.

"That used to be the Banca Italiana, but now it's going back to being Paul Revere's house. He was a famous man in this town, a patriot and silversmith."

"Like Cellini?" she said.

"Not so fancy as Cellini. Very simple. But very elegant. I'll buy you one of his bowls someday," he added.

Ten months after they married Marianna gave birth to their first child, Lucia Sicilia Cavallù. The following year Pacifico made his final payment to purchase the store — the business — he worked in, and three months later moved his growing family (another child, Marissa, had arrived) from their cramped two-room flat to the top apartment over the newly named P. Cavallù General Store. The store was the first floor of a three-story building of red brick. Pacifico painted the store's walls and ceiling a blazing white, added more lights, re-arranged the dry goods and brought in newspapers, sheet music and books. Business improved. The owner of the little building, Mr Samuel Levine, appeared every couple of months, a stout vigorous old man, exploring a roundabout route between the barrels, crates, crocks and boxes. "You're doing very well, Mr Cavallù. Whenever I come here you're busier than before. So many customers you have. You're prospering?"

Pacifico laughed. "You'll be raising my rent."

"*Not* Sam Levine. I want you to stay right here," he said, patting the counter and smiling. "So you can make lots of money and keep paying the rent on time. Unlike some people I know. —How are your little girls?"

One day, between customers, Pacifico asked him, "Have you ever thought of selling this building?"

"Have you ever thought of buying?"

"Me?" Pacifico looked surprised, operatically surprised. "No, no, no. I don't have the money to buy a building like this. —But if I did buy, I'd never have to pay rent for the store. I'd never have to pay rent for my apartment. And the tenants on the second floor would be paying their rent to me." He smiled.

"So you've thought of buying," Mr Levine said. He pressed the button on the tall gas-pipe cigar lighter and a short flame flared at the top. He leaned forward, lighted his cigar, let go the button and leaned back. "So I'll think of selling," he added. He exhaled a happy cloud of smoke, smiled and went out the door as two others came in.

A week later old Mr Levine walked in, paid for a cigar, slid a folded sheet of note paper across the counter, then angled his way between two customers and out the door. Pacifico looked at the dollar amount his landlord had written squarely in the middle of the little sheet, then he re-folded the paper, jammed it into his back pocket and went about his business, wondering all the while if he could raise such a sum of money. At the end of the day he sat down at the counter, took up a pencil and made a series of calculations on a flattened paper bag. The next morning he went around to the Shawmut Bank on Water Street, then to the Banca Italiana and then to an Italian money lender, and when he got back to the store he fished the note from his back pocket, drew a neat line through the Mr Levine's price and wrote a much lower number beneath it. Six days later, when Mr Levine was lighting his cigar at the gas jet, Pacifico slid the folded note back across the counter to him. Mr Levine tucked the note into his jacket's breast pocket, patted the pocket, and edged out through the throng at the door. A week later Mr Levine slid the note back across the counter to Pacifico. He'd drawn a line through Pacifico's bid and written a higher price below it. Nobody knows how many times the note passed back and forth between the two, but on the final occasion, just at closing time, Mr Levine slid the note to Pacifico, saying,

"I've come to the bottom of the paper. There's no more room. That's as low as I can go." He lifted his arms a bit and let them drop dejectedly to his sides, dramatically helpless.

As soon as they were alone, Pacifico unfolded the note — unfolded it carefully for by now the edges were frayed and one of the creases had torn — studied the dollar amount written at the base of that column of crossed-out sums. After a long minute Pacifico said, "Good!" and Mr Levine cried, "*Very* good!" and they shook hands vigorously. Pacifico gave a great laugh, snatched the stool from in back of the counter and gave it to him. Old Sam Levine seated himself with a grateful sigh and Pacifico Cavallù sat on an upturned crate, two plain drinking glasses and a dark bottle of wine between them. They drank. Sam winced, held up his glass and studied it, as if the color of the wine might explain the raw taste.

"Home made," Pacifico explained, clapping Sam lightly on the shoulder. "Sicilian!"

The older man hesitated, then tossed back his head, drained his glass and unbuttoned his vest. "Fine. Fine wine. — When I arrived here the North End was all Irish. Whiskey drinkers," he explained. "That was thirty, thirty-five years ago I arrived. Maybe longer. The years go by faster these days. The Irish were here but they were moving out. They needed to sell," — here he turned his left palm up — "we needed to buy," — he turned his right palm up. "We made deals." He clasped his hands. "The Irish had come up in the world and wanted to move out to the country, out to South Boston."

"I notice a lot stayed behind," Pacifico said, refilling the glasses.

"True." He signed. "A lot stayed behind and will never get out and even more moved in. The times are changing. I never thought the North End could be more crowded than what it was back then. But it's more crowded today."

"And now it's you moving up and moving out," Pacifico said.

Sam smiled and raised his glass. "First the Irish, then us, and next you."

That was early in 1908. By 1911 Marianna had given birth to Candida, which made four kids, and she had another rising in the oven — or maybe she already had five — and Pacifico had added more book shelves to the store, more clothesline with dangling sheet music, more cans of expensive tobacco and rows of fancy pipes, cigarette compacts, more tinted stationery paper and gold-nibbed fountain pens, mother of pearl picture frames, more fancy combs, hair brushes, pocket knives, large Italian playing cards, and he was now selling guitars, mandolins, harmonicas, player piano rolls, Victrola records, hand guns, ammunition, Venetian glassware and mirrors. He worked twelve and more hours a day, scanned the newspapers, took a book (biography, history, epic poetry) upstairs when he quit, washed up, ate dinner and played with the kids. Marianna, a baby at her breast, kept the accounts and prepared the meals. They still lived in the apartment (three windows up front, three windows in back) but nowadays Marianna sent the wash out and no longer had to haul on the pulley rope, heavy with damp or frozen clothes, and her fingers, which used to bleed that way, had healed. And by the time Dante was born, which made five — or maybe it was Sandro, which made six — they were able to hire Signora Bruno, who had been a scholar in Italy, to teach Lucia how to read Italian.

"God rested on Sunday," Pacifico told Marianna. "You can lie here or go to church. I alone, solitary and by myself, will do the cooking for the family," he announced.

Marianna sighed contentedly and settled back, her loose black hair uncoiled this way and that upon the pillow. "You cook beautifully, *caro*, but you don't clean up afterward," she said.

"Because I have to talk business with the men. Otherwise I'd never learn anything."

"Ah, yes. And what have you learned?"

"That I want to have a bank, the Cavallù Bank."

Marianna laughed, then stretched and sat up and saw his sober face. "Or are you serious?"

"Listen, I thank God I have a good back and two strong arms, but if I was still swinging a pickax we'd be living in a hole in the Maine woods. Now we have this store — we buy at one price and sell at a little higher price — and we have this building where we rent out one flat. We're doing well but our money is in mandolins and cigars and combs and in these brick walls. When I get my bank, my money will be in money."

"I can remember one day when you patted the front of this building. Remember? You said you liked to be able to reach out and touch your wealth. You said you liked it solid. Like *me*, you said and you tried to pat my culino. Remember?"

"You're right. I did." Pacifico reflected on it a moment, then laughed. "First I'll buy buildings, they'll bring in money, then I'll make my bank." He rolled out of bed onto his feet, the floor creaking under his weight. "Now, while you lie there recovering from our love making, I'll make you a café au lait." He pulled on his trousers, leaned into the crib to kiss Dante and already had one arm into his shirt as he walked out the bedroom door.

At those Sunday dinners they had Marianna's cousin Aldo and his Irish wife, and one of Pacifico's young journalist friends, and often doctor Balboni and his wife, or Bartolo, the lawyer, and his wife. When dinner was over and the women had gathered in the kitchen, the men would huddle at the head of the table to talk politics and finance. By the end of the year Pacifico had purchased the building at the corner of Prince and Hanover, a structure big enough to hold not only the expanding P. Cavallù store, but also an importing business, a travel office, a photographic studio and two or three other business he hadn't thought up yet.

By 1914 the Cavallù family had moved into a compact two-story wood frame house in Malden, a crowded town a few miles outside of Boston. It was an ordinary house with one step up to a broad front porch and another step up to the glass-paned door, on either side of which was a large window with a bright hand-painted shade (on the left, the Bay of Naples with Mount Vesuvius steaming in the background and on the right, the city of Messina with Mount Etna flaming in the background), and behind the glass door stood the grand rock of Monte Pellegrino, keeping guard over the placid blue harbor of Palermo. At Pacifico's direction, a squadron of carpenters and plasterers refashioned the front sitting room with crown molding, elaborate cornices and a fresh ceiling, and on that ceiling an artist — the same who had decorated the window shades — painted four acrobatic angels sailing skyward in a circle of vanishing perspective, their billowing garments of purple and gold trailing to the four corners of the room. It was in this house, at the top of the stairway to the second floor, that Molly had whispered *Fuck off!* to the banshee and poured water over her, and in this house that she recuperated after giving birth to Brendan. Of course, by then Marianna had given birth to Sandro, Silvia and, I think, Mercurio, making eight, and she wasn't through yet.

Pacifico's importing business had started years ago when he asked a cousin who was coming from Sicily to bring along as much popular sheet music as he could pack into the bottom of his suitcase. Now he had people in Palermo who bought whatever he wanted and every other month fifteen crates were unloaded onto the pier in Boston, trucked to

Cavallù Importing Company and dispatched from there to the shelves of Italian shops in Worcester, Providence and Hartford. The new travel office, run by the cousin who had brought the sheet music, was busy from the day it opened. The window displayed a three-foot-long ship model, a passenger vessel of the White Star Line, with finely detailed lifeboats, loading machinery, ventilation ducts and lounge chairs, one deck upon the other up to the great black funnel. Pacifico's daughter Bianca stood at that window one summer evening, marveling at the ship, and she remembered into old, old age how it looked when night filled Hanover Street and tiny lights inside the ship came on and the portholes, row upon row, shone over the dark sea.

Of course, no immigrant fresh off the boat was rich enough to make a voyage back to the old *paese*, but anyone could afford to send a picture showing how well they had done, so the photography studio always had customers. It was up a flight of stairs and down the hall, a room divided between a salon, with two large windows, and a laboratory or darkroom in which to develop and print the photographs. The salon had a bellows camera mounted on a tripod and two different canvas backdrops to choose from, plus a handful of props such as white paper roses or leather bound books, the most important prop being three dark vests (small, medium, large) and a glittering watch chain which signaled prosperity when draped across a vest.

∗ ∗ ∗ ∗ ∗

At first the Cavallù bank was no more than the black iron safe at the back of the P. Cavallù General Store on Prince Street, a safe big as a bedroom bureau and so heavy only Pacifico could move it. When you hauled open the iron door you found the store's tin cash box, a shelf of banged-up ledgers and a shoe box with a stack of envelopes containing bills, plus silver and gold coins, each envelope bearing the name of the depositor. The North End Italians were intimidated by the shimmering marble and glittering brass of Boston banks, and even if the frozen Yankee behind the barred window was polite — and how could you tell? — you never found out who was actually running the bank or where your money went when you slid it under the bars to the teller and, furthermore, they wanted a minimum deposit that was something like a month's wages. On the other hand, these depositors knew Pacifico Cavallù and were welcome at his store and they could see where he kept their money. You could go to him, show him your pass book and ask to see your cash. He'd bring you a little buff colored envelope with your name on it and your money inside.

"Can I count it?"

"Certainly. Go ahead and count it."

You could add up the bills and coins and see that it matched the sum in your passbook.

"How do I know this is my money, the money I

put in the envelope?"

"You just counted it," said Pacifico.

"But how do I know it's the *same* money I gave you."

"Does it look the same?"

"Yes."

"Exactly. It's the same," said Pacifico.

"When do I get the interest on my money?"

"After every three months. July is the next time."

None of the depositors had much money, but there were a lot of them and the little sums all added up, so by 1917 the words *Banca Cavallù* appeared in gold leaf on a new plate glass window on Hanover Street. The bank's board of directors included a grocer, a lawyer, a doctor, a newspaper editor, a café owner and a confectioner — each one a friend chosen for his business acumen and his willingness to trade his hard coin for paper bank stock at a hundred dollars a share. The bank made small loans to Boston Italians, sometimes without collateral, but Pacifico or one of the board members knew exactly the character and circumstances of every man the bank loaned to, and every loan paid off. By 1919 the bank had doubled its assets and the older Cavallù girls were enrolled in Notre Dame Academy, the school attended by Mayor Curley's daughters and the daughters of LaMarca who owned the Prince Spaghetti Company.

Then, in 1920, the devil himself turned up in Boston calling himself Charles Ponzi, a sharp dresser with a straw boater hat, a pinched waist jacket and glittering necktie pin. He tapped his walking stick on the pavement and announced the creation of the Securities Exchange Company which would make poor people rich. "Give me a hundred dollars today," he said. "And in ninety days I'll give you a hundred and fifty." Pacifico chose a jacket with threadbare cuffs and rode the subway downtown to the Securities Exchange Company's office on School Street. He said he was a clerk who wanted to invest, asked to see Mr Ponzi and asked him how the company could guarantee those remarkable profits. Mr Ponzi, smiling and relaxed, was happy to explain. "I used to be just like you," he said. "A hard-working man who was never able to get rich. Then one day I noticed that international postal coupons, which can be bought in this country for, maybe, a penny, can be sold in, say, Bulgaria for six cents. So I trade in international postal coupons, lots of them."

"Ingenious!" Pacifico said, breaking into Italian.

"And quite legal," Ponzi said, now in Italian too.

"And you share this secret method."

"Because I want others to enjoy being as rich as I am."

After a few more pleasantries, they shook hands and Mr Ponzi escorted him to the door. Pacifico returned to his bank, hung up his old jacket and put on his proper one, then he went home. "I visited Ponzi in his office today," he told Marianna. "The man is a fraud."

"You didn't have to go to his office to find that out," she said, taking the newspaper from him, a baby on her hip.

"I wanted to see what he looked like. He's thin, has no weight. I could pick him up with one hand and rattle him till his money fell all over the floor. He's going to ruin us."

"Calm yourself. Here. Hold Regina," she said placidly, handing him the baby. "By the way, have you thought about us moving to a bigger house?"

Word got around that Mr Ponzi was, as a matter of fact, paying his investors a fifty percent profit after only ninety days, just as he promised. Newspapers reported the astonishing success of the Securities Exchange Company and in no time investors began crowding into Mr Ponzi's office, their fists full of money. And many of those investors were withdrawing their savings from Banca Cavallù.

"You want to withdraw *all* your money?" Pacifico asked.

"Yes."

"Do you mind if I inquire why?"

"I'm going to make an investment."

"In Mr Ponzi's company?" Pacifico asked.

"I'd be a fool not to. So I need my money, all of it."

"Does anybody know this Ponzi? Does anybody know what place he comes from? Does anybody know his family?"

"All my money."

Pacifico sighed. "All right. Look. I'm giving you your money. Here. See? —This is silver. And this is gold, right? Now when you give this to Ponzi he's going to give you a promissory note printed on cheap paper and when you bring it back to his office in ninety days he'll be gone and your dollars will be gone, too."

"No. He's paying back in forty-five days now."

"Here. Go!"

Millions of dollars poured through the Securities Exchange Company as Mr Ponzi paid off his May investors with the money he was receiving from his June investors, and he paid off his June investors with the even greater sums he was taking in from his July investors. Dollars continued to drain from Banca Cavallù. Pacifico told his bank teller to step aside and he himself took over disbursing cash to his depositors, chatting amiably with each one and counting the bills and coins as slowly as he could. Banca Cavallù had $1507.30 in ready money when federal and state authorities closed in on Mr Ponzi, the Securities Exchange Company collapsed, and dollars began to flow again to Banca Cavallù.

"Listen," Pacifico said to Marianna. "You remember Cavagnaro who had a little bank in New York? He sold it to Giannini. And who is Giannini? Giannini is like me but he lives in California, which is a very long state, and he owns very many banks up and down that long state of California." Pacifico was standing at the bathroom sink, naked to the waist, whipping his shaving brush round and round in the shaving mug. "We can do the same thing here. First in Boston, then Rhode Island and Connecticut. What do you think?"

"What about the buildings on Unity Street?"

Marianna asked. She was in a pale yellow night-dress, standing at the door with Regina at her breast. "What about the buildings on Charter Street?"

"The buildings? What about them?"

"You haven't collected real rent from some of those tenants in months."

"We're doing fine. Attilio collects from each flat each month." Pacifico stopped abruptly, his shaving brush half way to his cheek. "Hasn't he been doing his job?"

"Attilio's an honest young man. He's also a gentleman and maybe too nice for the job. This month three different tenants put him off. He came away with an inlaid chess board, a silver candy dish and a parrot in a big brass cage.

Pacifico relaxed, laughed. "He's soft hearted. That's no sin. But I'll talk to him." He ducked past Marianna, his face covered with lather, and began cranking the gramophone.

"Fine. What am I supposed to do with all the junk he's collected?" Marianna said. "Attilio puts the rent money in your bank and brings everything else here. Where do you think the broken clock came from? We can't cram another thing into this house. We don't have enough room for the kids."

Pacifico returned to the sink, giving the baby a kiss and Marianna's buttocks a slap as he passed. "I'll buy us a bigger house," he announced. He swished his razor in the washbowl water and began to shave, pausing now and again to sing along with Caruso whose golden voice, sounding small and distant, floated up from the graceful horn on the gramophone.

* * * * *

So we come to the house where this chronicle ends and my biography begins. It was a big square three-story structure with a porte cochère on the left and a columned porch that traversed the front and wrapped around the right. (The villa in Italy also had three stories, but was built of stone, stucco and tile.) This was in Lexington where Paul Revere had roused the farmers, maybe a mile from the meadow where Aldo flew his newly built aeroplane back in 1910.

On the right of the Cavallù house in Lexington there were other broad lawns and large houses. On the left stood Saint Brigid's Catholic Church and beyond that, the parish house. And now comes the story I was told so many times I've got it word for word. It's 1930, it's early March, it's evening. It snows. Here comes the story. It comes *knock*, *knock*, *knock* by the heavy brass knocker on big front door. Then Pacifico pushes back his chair and gets up from the long table, his white linen napkin still tucked in his vest as he strolls across the big square hall and pulls open the front door. Outside it's all black sky and freshly fallen snow and, down at his feet, a large oval laundry basket with a mound of blankets and — "Good God!" he says. Now there's a clatter of dropped silverware and the scrape of chairs and everyone comes running to the door to get a look. They crowd the doorway but nobody moves — Pacifico is still peering into the dark where a few silent snowflakes tumble through the door light, then Marianna steps past him, cautiously lifts the basket and carries it on her hip to the dining room.

There were fifteen people in the Cavallù house that night — Pacifico, at this end of the table, a sturdy man of fifty with a short iron-colored beard, and Marianna at the other end, a mother with the full breasts and pelvic amplitude of a sea-woman carved on the prow of a sailing ship. Their children ran in age from ten to twenty-five and were known for being handsome, quick-witted and rash. They were seated on both sides of the long table — Lucia and Marissa and Bianca and Candida and Dante and Sandro and Silvio and Mercurio and Regina, along with Marissa's husband Nicolo, the aeronautical engineer, and Bianca's husband Fidèle, the stone cutter. And, of course, there was Carmela the cook and Nora the housemaid. That's two in the kitchen, thirteen at the table and me at the front door.

Mother Marianna shifted the wicker basket from her hip to her place at the table while everyone talked at once, saying he could have died out there and who would leave a baby in the snow and my God swaddling clothes and unwrap the poor thing and let's take a look. *Sfasciarlo! Sfasciarlo!"* - Unwrap it! Unwrap it! Then the women sang "Ah-ha!" And the men chorused "Oh-ho!" and Regina, the youngest, said, "Look at his little *ucellino*," while Mercurio, a year older, frowned and blushed.

"He's going to be strong," Pacifico said. "You can tell by the legs."

"A Calabrian," Marianna said. "They wrap them that way in Calabria."

"Mamà, they wrap them that way in Sicily, too," Lucia informed her.

"No. Not like that. That baby is Calabrese," her mother insisted. "He's been washed and rubbed with olive oil and then swaddled."

"That's terrible! I'm not doing that when I have a baby," Marissa said.

"Anyway, he wasn't born in Sicily or Calabria. He was born right here in Massachusetts," Lucia said.

The naked infant was nested back on the blankets in the wicker basket which was handed up over the espresso cups, crushed walnut shells and dried figs to Pacifico. The table quieted while he unhooked the watch chain from his vest, drew out the gold timepiece and lowered it delicately along side the baby's head, close by his ear. For a moment no one drew breath, then the infant turned toward the tick-tick-tick. Pacifico, his face still heavy with concentration, abruptly hauled the watch up and lowered it down the other side. Again the infant turned his head and twisted about to find the ticking. Pacifico, hoisted the watch once more and held it directly above the baby's face, rolling the chain between his fingers just enough to start the gold and crystal flashing. The infant stared up, fascinated. Pacifico slid the watch back into one of his vest pockets and looped the heavy gold chain across and then glanced up. "É bello," he concluded. "He's fine."

Marissa's husband Nicolo, that logical man, asked, "Did anyone look for a note?" Now everyone looked. They unfurled the blankets and shook them out, they went back through the big front hall and the vestibule to see if a little leaf of paper had dropped to the floor when they had trooped in, and they even went out onto the porch. There was no note. Regina had taken one of the blankets which wasn't a blanket at all, but only a cheap kerchief. "Look at this. Can I keep it?" she asked. It was a square of thin blue cotton printed with a fanciful map of Sicily, one of a thousand such kerchiefs. "How does it look?" she asked, pulling it around her shoulders and turning her head to see the effect. "What do you think? Can I keep it?"

"No. It doesn't belong to us," Pacifico told her. "And neither does the baby."

Marianna had taken the kerchief from her daughter and now she began to fold it. "Some poor confused woman didn't know which side of the church the parish house was on. If it wasn't so late we could take it over right now. Father McCarthy can find a home for it."

"Not Mr McCarthy," Pacifico told her. He refused to call any priest Father.

"All right. Father Basilio, then."

One by one they fell silent as they watched Marianna tuck the kerchief around the baby in the basket.

Carmela came and set a pan of warmed milk beside Marianna, looked without curiosity at the infant and then hobbled back to the kitchen. Nobody spoke. Bianca's husband Fidèle lowered his little finger into the baby's warm hand which closed tight around it.

"We can't give him back," Bianca said, breaking the silence. "We can't just give him *away!*"

"He belongs with his mother," big Marianna said firmly. "And his mother doesn't live here."

"But maybe the father is here," Candida said. "After all, it could be Dante or Sandro or —" She shrieked and ducked aside, as Dante lunged across the table to throw his wine in her face, Sandro already on his feet, his chair crashing backward. She swept the wine from her cheek with the back of her hand. "All I mean is —"

"Candida!" her mother cried.

"She talks too much!" Silvio said.

"You!" Dante said.

"Me? What about me?" Candida retorted.

"You know what about you," Sandro said.

"*Enough!*" Pacifico said, holding up his hand, palm outward.

The baby went on crying loudly in the sudden silence. Bianca swathed him in his blue map-kerchief and lifted him from the basket, cradling him in her arms, while her husband Fidèle brought up the pan of warm milk. He sat down beside his wife and sank a twisted corner of his napkin into the milk, saying, "He's a hungry boy. Let's give him something to drink."

* * * * *

I was adopted by Bianca and Fidèle who named me Renato, which means reborn, and here I am seventy-three years later, a man who doesn't know who or where he came from, writing a genealogical history of his family.

I've been told that every adopted child wants to find out, sooner or later, who his birth parents are but, frankly, I've never had that desire. What I know is that your true parents are the ones who bring you up, teach you your alphabet and your numbers, praise you and kiss you, or whack you when you misbehave, then they set you on your way and weep to see you go. Furthermore, like many kids adopted as infants, I grew to somewhat resemble my parents and people who didn't know better would say, "He has his father's looks," or "He gets those big eyes from his mother." I'm happy to say my mother was Bianca and my father was Fidèle, called Fred.

My father and his sister were orphaned when their parents died in the Spanish influenza epidemic of 1918. My father was nineteen and his sister Vivianna fourteen. My father took his father's place in the family, carving stone and cutting tile, while his kid sister kept house and did the cooking. At seventeen Vivianna married the man who had got her pregnant, but her baby died a few days later and her

209

husband took off. She worked here and there as a secretary, but after a few months she'd quit and take off, mailing her friends a stream of picture postcards by which they could chart her zigzag course down and up the coast or out to the Mississippi and back again. She even worked briefly for Pacifico in the summer of 1929 while my father and mother were on their wedding trip in Europe. Before my parents returned to Boston Vivianna went off and never came back. Her last postcard, mailed in 1930 from the minor honky-tonk town of Las Vegas, had a picture of the Hotel National, a bare two-floor shoebox with a striped awning over each window. *Here I am but not for long. Leaving for San Francisco on Monday & will write from there. Love to all, Viv.*

All my father ever said about Vivianna was that she was clever and restless. And, my mother added, she was attractive. Some years ago I found five snapshots of her forgotten in a stack of business documents in a large old envelope labeled *P. Cavallù & Co.* Two of the snapshots were taken indoors and they're dark; in one, Vivianna, her hair fashionably bobbed, sits in a swivel chair beside a broad black desk, and in the other she's by a window where the light leaves almost half her face in shadow. To be honest, they're lousy photos. The remaining three snapshots were taken out of doors on a breezy summer day. Her pale blouse opens wide at the throat and her hair blows across her cheek in a short dark crescent. The sun is bright and there's no blurring, even though she's turned her head and is laughing.

210

In this other snapshot she represses a smile, trying to hold still for the photographer, and in this last one — caught unaware, her skirt flapping in the wind — she's stepping down from a boulder to a beach, most likely the same beach that shows in the background of the other outdoor shots.

After I started writing this little book I began to look through the photos, letters, souvenirs and junk that got passed down the generations. I didn't come across anything new, nor was I able to fit everything together like a jigsaw puzzle. There were too many pieces missing. But I did notice that the man who ran the photography studio in the Cavallù building vanished the same time that Vivianna did. The photographer was Pacifico's half brother, Tancredi, the son of Pacifico's father, Fimi Cavallù, and a girl who worked in the kitchen — una picciotta di cucina — *not* Pacifico's mother, the passionate and learned Sonia DiSecco. Nonetheless, Sonia insisted that Tancredi, whom she had named, be brought up in the family and treated like any other Cavallù.

Tancredi was born in 1905, arrived in Boston in the summer of 1926 and left early in September of 1929. The story goes that he had always wanted to be a painter and that he had been driven crazy by having to photograph fat men in vests and a thousand little girls in First Communion dresses. The story also says that he didn't return to Sicily but went to Paris, and that might well be true. The only artifacts to survive from the studio are an ornate black oak chair and a French magazine, *La Révolution Surréaliste*, dated

October, 1927, with *Tancredi* scribbled inside the front cover. The cover was grimy, but the pages were clean and there was a startling photograph jammed deep inside — a naked young woman whirling away with something in her hand, maybe a blouse or a shift. Her arm and hand are blurred, her flying hair is trimmed just like Vivianna's and that slender back could well be Vivianna's too. The background is no help, a disheveled bed and an empty doorway.

Maybe Marianna was right and I was abandoned on the wrong doorstep by a confused woman who mistook this house beside the church for the one on the other side. Maybe it happened that way, a silhouette setting the basket ever so gently by the door, bending over it a long moment, then rising to knock, knock, knock and run away, glancing over her shoulder to see the door open and fill with light. If that's true, I thank my guardian angel who steered her to the Cavallù door. On the other hand, maybe Marianna was wrong and maybe the woman didn't mistake the grand Cavallù establishment with light pouring from every window for the tidy narrow gray parish house on the other side of the church, and maybe she knew very well at whose doorstep she was laying this infant. Maybe I resemble my mother and father because I'm the child of my father's wild kid sister and my mother's uncle. Or a man even more unlikely. Who cares?

I've never seen a photo of Tancredi, and all the family ever said of him was that he briefly managed the photography studio, fled to take up painting in

Paris, and that he was a *briccuni*, which is Sicilian for rogue or rascal or worse. As for Vivianna, for a short while she was a hectic young woman in family stories and now she's just an image in five Kodak snapshots and a blurred 7 x 9 photo used as a bookmark in a French magazine.

* * * * *

Pacifico and Marianna had nine children — Lucia, Marissa, Bianca, Candida, Dante, Sandro, Silvio, Mercurio, and Regina — and two homes, the big house in Lexington and the villa in Palermo. As it happened, the Second World War broke out while Marianna was in Massachusetts and Pacifico was in Sicily on business, and they weren't reunited until the war ended and Marianna sailed to Palermo. Pacifico died in 1948 after a good meal (melanzana con mozzarella), seated at his dining table with the plans of a cargo ship spread open in front of him. The villa had deteriorated, had leaky plumbing and loose wiring, and he'd rented out half of it, but he wasn't broke. On the contrary, he'd put together a group of like-minded friends and had acquired a surplus vessel from the United States Navy intending to start a shipping company. At this distance it's impossible to look over his shoulder to see if the ship was an LST, as some say, or a smaller craft. He died that summer day, his white beard pressed against his chest as if he were deep in thought, just before Marianna returned from the kitchen with his cup of espresso. As for Marianna, she lived long enough to welcome some of her grandchildren into the long garden behind the villa. She died early one morning in 1955, having seen her grandmother, the goddess, standing tiptoe on a big scallop shell that floated on the waters off the beach at Mondello, standing and beckoning as if she weighed nothing at all.

The Author

Eugene Mirabelli lives in upstate New York and writes for an alternative newsweekly. He is a professor emeritus (State University of New York at Albany) and was a founder and director of Alternative Literary Programs in Schools, a nonprofit arts organization to brings poets and storytellers into the classroom. In addition to his novels he has written short stories, articles and reviews.

The Typeface

William Caslon began to design typefaces around 1734 in England and his work quickly became popular throughout Europe and the Colonies. Benjamin Franklin admired Caslon's work and rarely used any other and, indeed, the first printing of the Declaration of Independence and the Constitution were set in Caslon. The version used here, Adobe Caslon Pro, was designed by Carol Twombly for Adobe Systems.